OUR PRECIOUS LULU

OUR PRECIOUS LULU

Anne Fine

ISIS
LARGE PRINT
Oxford

First published in Great Britain 2009
by
Bantam Press
an imprint of Transworld Publishers

Published in Large Print 2010 by ISIS Publishing Ltd.,
7 Centremead, Osney Mead, Oxford OX2 0ES
by arrangement with

TRANSWORLD PUBLISHERS

A Random House Group Company

The moral right of the author has been asserted

British Library Cataloguing in Publication Data
Fine, Anne.
    Our precious Lulu.
    1. Sibling rivalry - - Fiction.
    2. Stepsisters- -Fiction.
    3. Large type books.
    I. Title
    823.9'14–dc22

ISBN 978–0–7531–8504–9 (hb)
ISBN 978–0–7531–8505–6 (pb)

Printed and bound in Great Britain by
T. J. International Ltd., Padstow, Cornwall

For Richard, with love and thanks.

CHAPTER
ONE

He heard the door bang in that old familiar way, and even before Geraldine had struggled out of her coat she'd appeared in the doorway. "Guess what she's done now. Guess! Just guess! The bitch! The bloody bitch!"

The match was well into the second half, but still he forced himself out of his chair. "Want me to fetch you a drink? Then you can spit tintacks into it."

But Geraldine was in an even more distracted state than usual on these occasions. "No, no. Well, actually . . . Yes. Maybe I will."

"Red? White? A gin and tonic?"

"Oh, God! Red, please. No! White."

"Don't follow me out," he warned. "You know I have to take in the details of these dust-ups quite slowly, or I don't get them. You just sit there and blow your stack quietly to yourself till I get back."

By the time he brought in her drink, she had switched off the television. Bad luck on him. But he might catch the last few minutes of the game if she calmed down as fast as usual. (Poor lamb. She'd had enough practice.) "So," he said, putting the glass into Geraldine's hand and wrapping her fingers round it. "What has our precious Lulu done now?"

That set her off again. "The bitch! The bloody bitch!"

"I thought tonight was yoga. What can your sister possibly —"

"*Step*sister, thank you!"

"Well, what can she possibly do to upset you so much at a yoga class?" He ripped a bag of peanuts open with his teeth, then added, "Apart from sign up, of course," remembering how irritated Geraldine had been to find her sleek, bendy stepsister turning up at the very same sessions in which she herself had struggled for eight months.

"It wasn't *in* the class," said Geraldine. "It was right after. We all went off next door as usual, and got the big table. I reckoned that I needed to use the loo, so I went off. And when I came back, all of the rest of them were crowded round Lulu, crowing and patting her on the back and congratulating her, and all that crap."

"Oh, yes. All that crap."

"Don't you laugh! Wait till you hear. And everyone turned to me and said, 'Isn't it absolutely *wonderful*? Isn't it *brilliant*? You must be *thrilled* for Lulu!' And I suppose I must have looked completely baffled because suddenly they were all glancing at one another curiously and backing off, really embarrassed. I think they realized that I didn't know."

He wasn't sure that he was following. "Didn't know what?"

"What she'd just told them."

"Which was?"

"That she is pregnant."

2

"No!"

"Bloody bitch! Can't even pee on a stick and have the thing turn blue without somehow making it an opportunity to be vile to her own sister."

"*Stepsister*," he reminded her.

She wasn't in the mood for being teased. "Cow! Bitch!"

"Well, well."

They sat in silence for a while. Then Robert said, "Actually, you know, we've had a heap of crap from Lulu over the years. But I do truly think this takes the biscuit."

"Doesn't it?" said Geraldine. "Doesn't it *just*?"

And she burst into tears.

Crying is easier in the bath, so that's where she went. With her hair dripping down her face, she felt less leaky. Lulu had always been a venomous little baggage. Way back in primary school, before their parents had even met, let alone married, she had been brilliant at making others suffer. Geraldine would never forget the look on poor little William Webberley's face when he opened up what must have been the very first present he had ever been given in school, only to find a bit of dried-up dog turd in the box and hear Lulu's petty jeer, "Neh, neh! Fooled you!"

And when her stepsister wasn't playing horrid tricks, she was nasty in other ways. She was a positive expert in leaving people out. Geraldine herself had spent enough time trailing round the edge of the playground to know exactly what had happened to those poor creatures perpetually pretending to root for something in their schoolbags, and trying to look so indifferent when everyone knew that they were on the verge of tears and counting the minutes to the bell.

Thank God that Lulu had always been in a class one year group down. That eight-month gap in age had been a blessing, making things easier during weekends and holidays because they both had different friends. But still the two of them had spent enough time together to know one another backwards. So when the phone rang, Geraldine didn't reach over the edge of the bath to pick it up. She didn't want to hear her stepsister's smarmy pretence at innocence. "God, Geraldine! I am so sorry! I really, *really* didn't mean to —"

Bitch! How many years had Geraldine and Robert been trying to have a baby? Five, at the very least. Two on their own, two with the help of experts, and it was only six months or so since that tear-filled weekend when she'd decided that she couldn't stand it any more, and would he mind? And Robert had admitted he was relieved. He'd hated all that clinic crap. He'd loathed the fact that Geraldine was loading her system with chemicals. He kept on worrying she might get cancer and die on him. If she really wanted to adopt, then they could think about that. But, in the meantime . . .

The phone rang on. Let Robert pick it up downstairs if he chose. Geraldine didn't care how sharp he was with Lulu; she deserved it. But clearly Robert, too, thought better of tangling with his sister-in-law tonight.

4

Eight rings, and then the phone cut off with that half-chirrup that meant the answering machine was clicking in. And that was for the best. Robert had always known exactly when to say something and when to give things time. What was it Geraldine's mother had said about him so often over the years? "Dear Robert! Not much cop for looks, but so, so good with pets and toddlers."

And so, so good with wives. For he had always known how best to comfort her. After the last sequence at the hospital, he had been firm. "Out goes the whole damn lot!" Sure enough, all of that grisly and expensive paraphernalia had vanished overnight: the pamphlets, instruction details, timing devices and every last medication and syringe. "That's it!" he had declared. "We're free!" And suddenly the two of them were living in a whirlwind: weekend trips; New Year in Vienna; walking in Sicily; a fortnight in Goa. All of the things they wouldn't have dared to do with either a pregnancy or a small child. From time to time, held in his arms on dark nights, Geraldine did admit that there was still a painful yearning inside her somewhere. But it was getting better. At least they'd had the sense to be discreet all the way through, so there was no one in their circle of colleagues and friends who even knew about their disappointment.

Except for Lulu.

Oh, why had Geraldine been so stupid as to use that appointment card as a bookmark? Lulu had pounced. "What's this? Are you having treatment at this place? I didn't know!"

"No, no. I lent that book to Tania at work. She must have left that card in it."

"It's got your name on it."

So that was that, of course. Geraldine did try to play the whole business down, but she'd still had to tell at least a part of it. And Lulu had appeared all sympathy, and full of understanding. God knows what must have been in all those drugs that Geraldine had taken, to make her so soft-brained she thought that she might get away with it. No, not with dear Lulu's compulsion to seek out other people's soft places and stamp so casually and cruelly where it hurt most.

The bath water was stone cold now. Out she stepped, reaching for Robert's dressing gown because it was more comforting than her own. She came downstairs. "So. Have you listened?"

He didn't bother looking up. "Oh, yes. I listened. Don't even try because I deleted it."

"What was it, then? Don't tell me that she dared to say that she *forgot*?"

"No, no. It was some drivel about assuming that you'd take longer in the loo than you did. She was quite sure that by the time you came out the fuss would be over."

"Over? After a piece of news like *that*?"

"She claimed that when the rest of them had gone, she planned to take you somewhere quiet and tell you privately."

Geraldine pushed at the giant lump of purring fur that had been nesting on the sofa, then gave up and slumped down beside it. "She is extraordinary, isn't she? You really wouldn't think that someone who's so good at being spiteful could think up such half-baked excuses."

"But that's deliberate, surely."

"You think so?" The notion took Geraldine by surprise. "Put down that paper and say that again."

He dropped the paper on the arm of his chair and reached for his beer can. "It's perfectly simple. I think that Lulu is forever trying to push you over the edge. She gets her jollies out of sticking pins in everyone, and I think it really irritates her that you never lose your temper. You always forgive her."

"I *never* forgive her."

"Well, *I* know that. But she doesn't, does she? Because you make an absolute fetish of never offering her the satisfaction of seeing how upset you are. You've always responded that way." He took a swig of his beer. "This evening, for example, in the café. What did you do?"

She blushed. "Pretended I'd noticed a traffic warden prowling round my car. Then I fled, hurling apologies behind me."

"See? And Lulu thinks she simply hasn't prodded hard enough. So she gets worse and worse, and turns each half-arsed explanation or apology into even more of an insult. I reckon all she wants is for you, just for once, to crack."

"Crack?"

"You know. Act like a normal person. Burst into tears. Yell at her. Slap her face. Anything."

"Then she might knock it off? You really think that?"

7

"Yes, I do. Why else would she waste her time dumping this sort of vileness on to you time and again? She's jealous. Jealous because you have a decent husband and she only has that daft Harvey — when he's not back with his wife. Jealous because you have a sensible career, and she just flits from one silly job to another. Jealous because you're nice and she is nasty. Jesus! Here, hide the last of these peanuts before I end up as fat as that damn cat."

She tucked what he'd left of the packet safely behind a cushion, then pulled it out again. Soothed by the ebb and flow of Puffer's purr, she munched away for a while. Jealous — of course. That didn't come as news. Didn't they all remember the time that Lulu started on about the posture badge? All Robert had said when he came round to their house after school prize-giving was, "Geraldine did well, then!" And Lulu had been out of her cage. "I got the Posture Badge!"

Their big mistake was thinking she had made a joke. And since Lulu didn't have much of a sense of humour, perhaps they'd laughed a little too enthusiastically, because she'd flared up. "What is so funny about that?"

Geraldine's mother had wiped the smile off her face in a flash. "Nothing, dear. Nothing."

"So why are you all laughing?"

No one could think of any good reason — except, of course, that it was funny to compare scooping up all three of the sixth-form science prizes with getting "Posture". Robert had pitched in as usual to try to deflect the flack. "So what is posture anyway? What does it *mean*?" He'd made a great performance out of saying the word in a pretentious manner. "Poss-chure! Poss-chure! Is it just standing up straight?"

"Of course not!" Lulu snapped. "It's about the whole way you hold yourself and how you behave, and your attitude and everything."

Even mild Mrs Carter had found herself baulking a little at this. "No, I don't think so, dear."

And Lulu lost her temper. They'd had the works. The flashing eyes and stamping feet. "It is! It is! Don't try to tell *me* what it is. I won it! And it means a whole lot more than just stupid sitting up straight. It's *just* as important as physics, biology and stupid, stupid *maths*!"

Embarrassed to their very bones, no one had pointed out that Geraldine's third prize had been for chemistry. And that was the problem, of course. Nobody tangled with Lulu. Some held back out of fear, and some from pity. And others were simply too unsure of what might happen, because it truly did seem as if within her boiled some outlandish force that might at any moment set her off down a track everyone would regret.

So no one tackled her, and ugly scenes came thick and fast. It was as if, over the years, Lulu had managed to train them all to put up with anything — anything — rather than risk another barrage of her desperate hysteria. The only dignity that Geraldine had been able to snatch from these unsavoury occasions had been the satisfaction of flattening all expression, pretending to be deaf to every insult, and, best of all, popping her head around a door only a few minutes later with a casual, "Lu, seen my pencil sharpener?", or, "I can't remember whether you said you were coming into town this afternoon with us or not?" Anything simply to rob her stepsister of the satisfaction of knowing how hard she had struck.

Posture badge, though! It was ridiculous. Crumpling the empty peanut bag, Geraldine tossed it across the room at the waste-paper basket. It missed, and rolled along the carpet, spilling salt.

"Crap shot," jeered Robert.

"I wasn't trying," she defended herself. "And I already *know* that Lulu's jealous. That's how I keep from letting fly and scratching her eyes out. The trouble is, I'm not sure I can carry on. I think I'm finally ready to give up and take your advice."

"Everyone's advice, not just mine. Your friends. Your colleagues. That weirdo therapist woman. *Everyone.*"

"Except for Mum."

"Well, yes. But your mother has a vested interest in keeping you at it, doesn't she? I mean, if you decide that it's not worth the candle trying to placate that vindictive little minx any longer, and make a go of cutting loose, then Jane will have to start to ask herself why she's let Lulu chew up so much of her own life."

Geraldine sighed. "Oh, well. That's her problem now. Because I think I'm ready to write a letter to Lulu telling her I never, *ever* want to see or hear from her again."

There was a long, long silence while both of them considered the fact that toughness of this sort had never been Geraldine's strong suit. If she'd been halfway capable of keeping any resolution of this sort, she would have written the letter years before.

"But, on the *other* hand . . ." said Robert suddenly.

She turned her head to see a smile she didn't recognize. "On the other hand, what?"

Now he was grinning, as if he'd suddenly snapped back into himself. "Just that it almost seems a shame to quit now, while you are so far ahead, and she has been so nasty. If you were *ever* going to crack and let fly back at her, it would have been tonight. So don't you feel a tiny, tiny bit like making the most of your laurels?"

"What do you mean?"

"Well, paying her out, I suppose. Making a hobby of it."

"A *hobby*?"

"Why not? That's what she seems to do to you, after all. She just gets on quite happily with her own life and then, whenever she gets bored or you provoke her —"

"I don't provoke her!"

"Yes, you do. You know. By getting promotions and awards and things."

"Oh, *that* sort of provoke."

"Yes. That sort. That always seems to be when she sets up these little stabbings in the back. She gets at you by being foul. You parry by appearing not to notice, or not to mind." He shook his head in wonder. "It's like a psychic sword fight. You two are in a little personal Shakespeare play all of your own. So take her on. Stay unperturbed — *whatever*."

"To what particular purpose?"

It was as if he hadn't quite thought this bit through. But in the end he came up trumps with something heartening.

"Revenge, of course. What else? I told you, it's like a play. In the last act, she will go mad and die. We'll say a few improving words over her body, and have the bloody little bitch out of our lives for ever."

CHAPTER
TWO

It wasn't like her Robert. Brooding about it later in bed in the dark, Geraldine wondered if, to him, this business of not being able to have a baby had been a good deal more upsetting than he'd let on. It would be typical of him to cover up his own real feelings in order to save her from feeling worse. She couldn't think of any other reason why he would do a total turnabout on all his usual advice: "Just give the venomous little madam one more clear warning, and then as soon as she misbehaves again we'll freeze her out."

(Or follow his own family to Australia without leaving any forwarding address. That had been one of the other solutions he had suggested, and Lord it was tempting in spite of their good jobs and her perennial anxieties: "But it's so far away!" "We can't *both* walk out on the lab at the same time," and, of course, "What about my mother?")

But to suggest that they just carried on dealing with Lulu as they had always done before? That was so odd.

There again, people were always surprising you. Look at the way her mother had allowed Lulu back in the house after the divorce. Jed's drunken crash had put an end to that short paradise in which their home had once again descended into sweet, sweet calm. In the few intervening years there had been contact, of course. The two of them had made a point of sending gifts for Lulu's birthday and at Christmas. ("It's not as if her father's any good at celebrations — unless, of course, they include making a dent in a bottle.") But neither of them ever spoke of missing her. It had been such a shock to hear the news. "What?" Geraldine remembered asking. "She's coming back to live with us again? For *good*?"

"I think so, yes."

"But *why*? We're not her family any more. It's not our fault Jed died. Why do *we* have to have her?"

"I know it seems a little odd. But I don't really see where else Lulu can go. I did ask round after the funeral. There are a couple of great-aunts. But the one who took Lulu's mother back to Lima when she got ill has never bothered to come back again. And the other looked positively dreadful. You wouldn't want Lulu to have to go to her."

"Why not?"

Jane Carter shuddered. "Honestly, Geraldine. Just take my word for it. She has to come to us. At least till she's sixteen."

And that was that. Lulu was back. She'd barely changed. Indeed, she'd obviously spent the years they'd been apart honing her knack for making everyone around her feel one inch tall. If Geraldine so much as glanced at a boy, then two days later Lulu would be telling her which leggy, pencil-thin blonde he was already dating. When Geraldine's skin broke out, Lulu would sit beside her on the bed suggesting creams and lotions, and sympathizing so strongly that Geraldine felt each blemish on her face must be enormous. And what about the day Geraldine had come home dancing on air to tell her mother and her stepsister that handsome, gorgeous Akil Baksar in the year above had pulled her aside towards the end of break and asked her if she'd like to have his second ticket to a gig on Saturday. Her mother had been delighted for her. "Oh, Geraldine! That's lovely!"

Lulu said nothing. For a few blissful moments, thrills of excitement ran through Geraldine. Could Lulu — pretty, slim, and much admired by all the boys — finally be jealous of her?

It was a pleasure that couldn't last. The moment Mrs Carter had left the room, Lulu was leaning over the table and asking with tender concern, "Akil *Baksar*? Oh, Geraldine, are you quite *sure* he meant a proper date?"

The germ of doubt that Lulu introduced gnawed throughout the week. Uncertain of herself, Geraldine took care to stay away from Akil in every corridor and through every break. She wouldn't meet his eye. What if he'd only wanted to offload the ticket and thought that she, of all the girls in the class, was the most likely to be at a loose end on Saturday night? What if the right thing to do was bring in money and take the ticket from him now, as if it were a simple and sensible transaction? What if the whole suggestion were just some dare, and boys from the year above would all be lurking, sniggering, in the dark outside the arena, watching her as she wondered how long to stand there pretending to take an interest in the small print on the back of her ticket, waiting and waiting?

By Wednesday, Akil was avoiding her as much as she was hiding from him. On Thursday, he talked loudly in the classroom about a sudden family funeral and up came poor squat Johnny Fuller, waving both tickets and barely trying to hide the fact that he'd been bribed to act as substitute by being given his own for nothing. Geraldine had her pride and, in a flurry of sick notes to school and messages to Johnny, saved face by spending Friday and Saturday reading in bed. And all the practice at avoiding Akil's eye had come in useful later, when Lulu floated round the house with that great smirk of triumph on her face.

And it had been pointless, trying to cling to the notion that this small private hell would only last for two more years. Even back then, Geraldine had known that "till she's sixteen" was just another of her mother's soft evasions. What was Jane Carter planning to do, for heaven's sake? Hand over an especially lavish gift on Lulu's birthday, then say, "Well, there you are. We've done our bit for you. Now pack and go"? The fact is, Lulu was pretty much a proper orphan, and they comprised her only half-real family. She had to stay. And though, whenever she played the drama queen or fell into one of her prodigious sulks, Geraldine presumed her mother found this mutinous cuckoo almost as tiresome as she did herself, nothing was said. Suddenly the two of them were back once again to acting the parts of caring and loving people under their own roof.

That was what made the entrance of Robert into their family life such a relief. The day the Forsley family moved in next door, he'd been sent round — a gangling, awkward youth, disfigured with acne — to borrow a broom. Lulu could barely hide her contempt, and even Geraldine had probably shown her disappointment that the owner of the smart racing bike they'd seen unloaded from the van only an hour before could fall so far short of their hopes.

Off he had gone, bearing the filthy horror their mother had been almost ashamed to offer him. When it came back it was a different beast, the handle scrubbed clean and the bristles shining.

Jane Carter was embarrassed. "Honestly, you shouldn't have!"

He stayed for supper that night, and the next. And on the way to school on Monday morning, he had caught up with Geraldine and walked beside her.

"God, but your sister's *scary*."

She said the words she'd never dared spit out so fiercely before: "She's *not my sister*."

"Phew!" he had said. And that was all. But still it seemed to flick some sort of switch, letting back into her heart a little of the confidence that had been slipping away since Lulu's return. That was the thing about Robert. Just like her stepsister, with one word he could change a mood — except that, in his case, it was generally to make things better and not, as in Lulu's, always worse.

Apart from a couple of hours before when, on the way up to bed, she'd asked him suddenly, "Do you suppose that she's told Mum?"

He was still glancing back towards the silent cat flap. "About the pregnancy? Of course."

"How come you're so sure?"

He forced his attention back from the wayward Puffer. "Think it through, Geraldine. If she's prepared to make you look a fool in front of people you only meet at yoga, she's scarcely going to pass up the satisfaction of arranging things so you're the last in the family to hear the news."

"So why didn't Mum tip me the wink when I called in on her on the way to class?"

Giving up on the unfaithful Puffer, Robert followed his wife up the stairs and into the bedroom. "I expect she was under orders. Oh, Lulu will have taken care to make it sound all sisterly and caring: 'Now don't you say a word to Geraldine! I want to tell her myself.' But it will just have been another little power trip."

"You really think so? Because I think, if the situation was reversed and Lulu had just told *me*, I wouldn't have been able to sit with Mum and not even hint there might be something in the wind."

"That's why the teasing only works in one direction." He'd put an arm around her waist and pulled her closer. "All part of Lulu's fun. When are you going to realize that Lulu treats your mother like a knight in chess? She is forever sending Jane two squares to the front and one to the side."

"Mother's not stupid."

"No," he'd agreed. "And sometimes, like this evening, she isn't kind."

She hadn't argued. One of the things they'd had to learn to disagree about was how Jane Carter responded to Lulu and her wiles. To Geraldine it usually seemed as if her mother were on the run — outsmarted by a girl who, from the cradle, had been pulling wires. To Robert it was obvious that Mrs Carter always chose the option that caused least trouble, which, since her own child was a gentle soul, meant Lulu won hands down in any contest. "People like Lulu end up ruling the world," he'd grumbled more than once. "Especially when people like your mother acquire the knack of acting as if each little act of spite is just some accident best ignored, and not the last redoubt."

The last redoubt! She'd teased him for the sheer pomposity of the phrase. But it had stuck in her mind. There had been so many times when she'd looked back and thought, "*That* is the moment when Lulu should have been pulled up." But, to be fair, she'd been no braver herself. Even when she'd seen Lulu-isms coming, she'd simply laid her neck across the block and waited. Look at the night before her very own wedding. Lulu had sprawled across the bed, playing the part of the supportive sister. "So! Twelve more hours and you'll be Robert's wife! When did you first decide to marry him?"

"It isn't like that, Lu. You don't just set your sights on someone and pick them off."

Lulu had let out a dramatic sigh. "Oh, suit yourself. I'll ask a different way." She held out an imaginary

19

microphone and simpered, "Tell me, Miss Prim, when did the idea first pop into your head of marrying Robert Forsley?"

What sort of fool had Geraldine been to answer so frankly? "In a biology lesson."

"You're joking! What were you doing, for heaven's sake? Mooning across the room, admiring his spots?"

"Oh, shut up, Lu!"

"Sorry! I didn't mean to say that. Carry on."

And Geraldine was trapped. If she had broken off the conversation in a huff, Lulu would bait her for sulking. And though she was well aware that what she was about to say was almost certain to invite more ridicule, she felt uneasy about telling any sort of lie on this of all nights. "If you must know, we were studying proportions of body fat."

She waited for the contemptuous snort, but Lulu just looked blank. Of course, her track record at school had been so poor that she'd been shunted into Combined Sciences. Maybe she didn't know. "It's just to do with the different ways that men and women store fat. You get a pair of callipers —"

"*Callipers?*"

"Not that sort. Pincers, to take a bit of flesh and measure it." Even now, Geraldine could remember she'd taken care to pull her stomach in before she'd dared to lift her blouse and demonstrate with fingers. "Like this."

Lulu had shuddered. "God! How embarrassing!" She'd grinned. "Especially for the *real* fatties."

20

Why had she laid that emphasis on the word "real"? It might have been entirely innocent. But still it was enough to bring all Geraldine's anxieties about her choice of wedding outfit straight back to mind. Forcing down panic, she'd pressed on with the story. "Yes. Especially for them. Mr Denby kept saying the word 'fat', and people were sniggering. Poor Brenda Kottler was pretty well in tears."

"And how did *you* come out of it?"

"I can't remember," Geraldine had lied. "But individuals didn't matter anyway because he was comparing boys with girls, and all the boys were practically stick insects."

"What's all this got to do with Robert?"

She could remember wondering, even at that point, whether or not to go on. It sounded so stupid — not at all a reason for thinking someone was the sort of person you'd one day want to marry. But there was Lulu, sweetly picking counterpane fluff off one of Geraldine's sleeves, and looking all sincere.

And she was only back for that one night, before the wedding.

"It was more afterwards, really. I think that everyone was on edge when we packed up to leave. We knew there'd be teasing. You know the sort of stuff: 'With you on their side, Kottler, we lads never stood a chance!' I think that one or two of us were even thinking of hanging back so we could protect her."

Geraldine could see it now. That drab old classroom with the nasty dark-wood cabinets. The ancient posters on the walls. The grungy box in which they dropped their lab coats. And, behind those, the double doors where she had fallen in love because this Robert who'd moved in next door only a few months before suddenly leaned across to whisper something to the boy beside him at the bench. As soon as Mr Denby said the magic words, "All right, then. Off you go," the two of them were on their feet and rushing for the doors. Neil took one side, and Robert took the other. In seconds both the catches were up, the doors wide open and the boys standing like sentries. "Room enough, ladies? Can you get by? Is it quite wide enough? We could try pushing back the doors a little more if there's a problem!"

She felt a rush of warmth for him even as she retold the story to Lulu. How everyone had piled through, even poor Brenda, who had so cleverly been transformed from a humiliated fat girl into just one more in a noisy gang of pupils being teased. The moment most of the class were through the doors, Robert and Neil had rushed ahead down the long corridor to repeat the performance at the far end. Floor catches up, wall hooks flipped on, and endless noisy expressions of concern lest female classmates had some difficulty getting through a gap at least two metres wide. Such a good joke, the boys had carried on almost all term, with teachers mystified to see their pupils leaping up in pairs from lunch tables to hold both dining-room doors wide open for some thin wraith who could quite easily have lost herself inside a cucumber sandwich.

And what had Lulu said when Geraldine had finished?

"Oh, *I* see."

Just, "Oh, *I* see." But somehow she had put a world of meaning into it, as if to say, "So *that* is why you fell so hard for him. Because he's really, really good with people who are overweight."

Geraldine rolled over in bed, and poked her husband gently. "Are you awake?"

He offered her his usual mild response. "Well, I am now."

She cuddled closer. "Robert, I'm lying here thinking and I've decided that you're right. We shouldn't change tack now. I won't give Lulu the satisfaction of thinking she's upset me. Especially not about this. So I am going to face her out."

He squeezed her. "Quite right! Tomorrow morning we shall plan our counter-attack."

Comforted, Geraldine burrowed down while Robert kept on staring out, into the dark. He was surprised it hadn't taken her a whole lot longer to agree with him, and lay awake for quite a while wondering why. So it was not surprising that, as he finally drifted off towards his own dreams, he was not sure if he imagined it, or if he really heard her muttering the words that seemed to skitter through his mind.

"See how far she dares go. Winner takes all."

CHAPTER
THREE

At nine o'clock the following morning, the phone rang. Robert picked up. It was his mother-in-law. He launched in first. "Jane! I hear congratulations are in order and you're to be a granny!"

He'd chosen his words with care. It might seem mischievous, but hadn't he had to sit by and watch while Mrs Carter sacrificed her own daughter's sense of ease in her own home by her refusal to recognize that taking on Lulu a second time had been a big mistake? What was so awful about taking malicious delight in hinting that she couldn't really pick and choose now? Too bad if, at this stage in life, she would prefer a little peace and quiet. "Your very first grandchild!" he chortled. "*Marvellous!* You must be absolutely thrilled."

"It's *lovely*, isn't it?" she said, before as good as confirming their suspicions of the night before by adding, quite unnecessarily, "Of course, I've only just heard."

I'll bet! he thought. But all he said was, "Wonderful!" He chose the bracing tone to pay her out for all those hundreds of occasions he'd sat across their kitchen table and wondered why she didn't turn on Lulu and

24

warn her, "Listen, young lady. This is my Geraldine's home as much as yours. More, really. And if you can't stop needling her, I think perhaps I should phone your aunt in Lima and you can see if you get on better there."

So let Jane Carter wince at the thought of yet another twenty years, or more, of being tied to Lulu. It served her right. "*Won't* it be nice for you," he persisted, "to have a brand-new baby in the family!"

It was as if she brushed this last aside. "Robert," she almost whispered, "I'm glad it wasn't Geraldine who picked up the phone. There's something I'd quite like to ask, entirely in confidence."

He waited. It was some time before she spoke again. "By the way, where is Geraldine? Could she be hearing this?"

"No, no. She's off in town."

"Already? It's a bit early, isn't it?"

He forced out a chuckle. "Probably already buying baby clothes!"

"Well, that's the point, really. I wanted to ask you — well, the two of you, of course. But it's easier to speak to you first. I wanted to know how Geraldine is feeling about this business."

By Christ, the woman had a nerve, keeping Lulu's mean little secrets, then trying to pretend she was concerned the news might have come as a shock.

"Sorry," he said. "Not sure I'm following."

"This business of Lulu's being pregnant, of course. I mean, does Geraldine mind?"

Robert affected bafflement. "Mind?"

"Is she . . .?" It took Jane Carter only a moment to repress the word "jealous" and offer the far more tactful, "Is she at all disappointed on her own behalf?"

He wasn't going to make it easy for her. "How do you mean?"

"Well, you know. About not having babies of her own."

"*Our* own."

"Of course. That's what I meant." Since he had left her dangling, she pressed on. "So, dear, is she?"

"What?"

"For heaven's sake! This isn't like you, Robert. Surely you understand what I'm saying. Is this big news of Lulu's something that's likely to upset Geraldine?"

Likely to? What sort of dream world did the woman live in? But it was better not to pick her up on that. Already he had pushed his luck almost too far. Stick to the plan. "Oh, sorry! I see what you mean! For just a moment I wasn't on your wavelength. You're wondering if we ourselves were hoping to start a family."

"I know it seems horribly nosy. But, what with this news of Lulu's coming out of the blue, I simply wanted to assure myself that —"

"Honestly, Jane! No problem." And out they poured, the lies he'd honed to slick perfection in the sleepless dark. "There was a time a couple of years ago when we tried hard to think ourselves into the business. As I recall, Geraldine even had a couple of appointments at one of those clinics that offer some blood test that tells you how long you can leave things before you have to make up your mind." He dropped his voice to sound more confidential. "I shouldn't be telling you any of this, of course. As you know, Geraldine is very, very private about this sort of thing. But since you're worrying, I think it's better that I put your mind at rest."

"You can be very sure that I'll respect your confidence, Robert."

"I'd be grateful for that. Don't want to end up in the dog-house! But frankly, the long and short of it is that, in the end, the two of us decided we were a bit too selfish for the whole caboodle. Once we had forced ourselves more or less up to the fence, as it were, we baulked at the last minute."

He waited while his mother-in-law processed his version of events. "But Lulu seems to think —"

"Oh, Lulu! Well, I do remember Geraldine telling me the two of them had had a conversation on the matter and she thought Lulu might have got rather the wrong end of the stick. But then she wondered whether Lulu was perhaps projecting a little. You know — a whole lot keener on the idea for herself than she let on."

"Really?"

"Yes."

Go on, he told himself. Have fun. Put in the boot. "But that, of course, was straight after one of those times when Harvey's wife had thrown him out, so maybe things were all a bit unsettled."

He couldn't see her wince, but he could have the pleasure of imagining it. And now: the coup de grace! "And Harvey must be quite delighted too. What will this be? Is it his fourth child? Or just his third?"

To his great satisfaction, her voice was faint. "But surely Harvey only has the twins . . ."

"His third, then. He'll be so pleased. But then, we *all* are, aren't we? And you must all come round to celebrate the happy news. How about supper tonight? Don't even think of bringing anything. We'll do the lot. You just ring Lulu and Harvey and tell them to come at seven, will you? Thanks!"

Geraldine was home within the hour. "Dear Christ, this town is bloody."

"You shouldn't go."

"We have to eat."

"But I have to go shopping anyway. Everyone's coming round to celebrate tonight."

She put down her bags and stared. "Really? Did you invite them?"

"I'm sorry. But it had to happen." He stifled his smile to stop her guessing how much he had just enjoyed baiting her mother. "Jane rang, and suddenly there seemed no choice but to bite the bullet."

She sighed. "Oh, well. So long as I don't have to do it all."

"No, no. I'll shop and cook. And we'll cheat on the pudding."

"It's a deal. Is Harvey coming?"

"Hope so."

She burst out laughing. "You are *terrible*. You just enjoy tormenting the poor man."

"He's such a *wimp*."

"You should feel sorry for him. The poor sap's stuck with Lulu now."

"I can't feel sorry for Harvey."

And it was true. Everything about the man made his flesh creep. The way he hung back in doorways, letting in the draught, until you almost physically pulled him in. His flabby handshake and pathetic inability either to contribute anything of interest to any topic under discussion, or take the initiative to start up a new one. In his own slow-moving, pleasant-looking way, Harvey was a big nothing. ("Still waters running shallow," as Jane once said in deep exasperation.) And the way he had dumped his wife and family the very first time had filled them all with deep disgust.

Lulu had rung one night. "Geraldine, guess what! Harvey is finally leaving Linda. He's moving in tomorrow."

Geraldine had tried to put on the brakes without offending Lulu. "Really? Are you quite sure you want to share your flat? People can be quite tiresome at the end of a marriage. It might be better for him just to rent a place of his own for a while — give everyone a sort of firebreak."

"No, no. It'll be fine. He barely spends any time at home as it is, and even then it's only so he gets to see the twins. Anyhow, he's psyched up now. He's telling Linda tonight. That's why I've rung you. I'm like a cat on hot bricks."

Geraldine had glanced with longing at the piles of work stacked on the table. "Want to come round?"

Reprieve! "God, no. I'm staying here in case she hurls him out with all his socks and underpants flying out after him. It should be a good laugh."

"Lulu, it won't be easy. After all, there are the children . . ."

"Oh, don't you worry about them. They're far too young to have a clue about what's happening."

"Lulu —"

But she'd hung up. Next day there was no word. No, nor the next. In the end Geraldine had rung her mother. "Have you heard anything from Lulu?"

"No, dear. She told me Harvey was moving in some time this week."

"Friday, she said."

"Where are we now? Sunday. I haven't heard a thing."

"Perhaps it worked out all right."

"I expect it did."

It hadn't, though. Later, between the three of them, they'd pieced the story together: how Harvey had gone home that evening only to find his wife practically in tears over a bowl of egg whites. "I must have got yolk in here. They just won't whip. Harvey, you'll have to nip down to the corner shop and buy another dozen."

"Can't it wait?"

"Wait?" It seems that Linda had looked up and said sarcastically, "Oh, yes! Of course it can wait — if you can put off all six of the people we invited for supper tomorrow. Which would you rather, Harvey? Make a lot of embarrassing phone calls, or nip down to KeenKost?"

30

"Blimey!" said Robert when Lulu, under persistent questioning on her next visit, had filled in the details of the tale. "Had the man simply *forgotten*?"

Lulu had defended her lover. "I don't think that's so odd. They entertain a lot. Linda likes cooking. And I think it's quite decent of Harvey to change his mind at the last minute and decide not to tell her till after their dinner party."

Behind her back as he refilled her glass, Robert had rolled his eyes upwards. "Heavens, yes. Much the most decent line to take. Positively noble."

"Oh, you can scoff," said Lulu. "You two are such a boring couple, you *never* have people for dinner."

"Excuse me," Robert rebuked her. "I think you'll find you're eating our grub now."

"Only because I'm *family*."

That was so true that Geraldine had rushed to move the conversation on. "So what's going to happen now?"

"He's going to try again."

"When?"

"This coming Thursday."

Robert leaned over gallantly to hand Lulu her fresh glass. "Is there some subtlety I don't know," he asked, "about the etiquette of leaving your wife and family? Is Thursday the only day of the week on which it should be done?"

Lulu had swiped at him affectionately. "Daftie."

Safe in bed after she'd gone, they had discussed the matter. "Are we just *awful*?" Geraldine had asked the darkness round them. "Mean-spirited and moralistic?

I mean, marriages do break up. So maybe Lulu's right, and if the twins are really young, it will be easier for them."

"Maybe. You couldn't shift your knee off for a bit? My leg's gone dead."

"That's not my knee. That's Puffer."

"By Christ, he's heavy."

She waited while he pushed at the idle furry lump. "Move, you great podge! This is our bed, not yours!" After she'd heard the sullen thump as Puffer hit the floor, she took up her defence of Lulu's boyfriend. "And why not put it off till after some dinner party you've forgotten you were having? I mean, I know it sounds repellent and ridiculous to keep on living a lie for even a few more days for something so trivial. But in a way it makes a kind of sense."

"Yes," Robert said. "Like putting off a crucifixion till the weather's better."

And they had rolled together and made love.

CHAPTER
FOUR

Mrs Carter arrived first. "Robert! How lovely to see you. It feels as if it has been *weeks*." She hugged her daughter. "And you, Geraldine. You're looking lovely. Is that a new skirt?"

"No, no," said Geraldine. "Come and sit down and tell all, quickly, before the other two arrive."

"Tell all? What do you mean?"

"You know. How pregnant *is* she? Is Harvey really pleased or simply faking it? Has he told Linda and the twins? Can they afford it? Will she keep working?"

She took some pleasure in watching her mother's fingers writhe in her lap. "Well, I don't know, dear. Surely these are questions you should be asking Lulu, not me."

"I can't ask Lulu! How can I ask Lulu? These are the questions only family can answer."

"You're family too, dear."

"I didn't even know that she was *trying* for a baby."

Jane Carter bridled at any of her daughter's small, stubborn reminders that years of sharing a home had led to no true intimacy between the two of them. "I'm not sure that she was. You know how these things happen. And as for how far gone she is, it can't be much. She certainly hasn't begun to show."

"A winter baby, then. Maybe not even until after Christmas."

"We'll have to ask her."

"We most certainly will."

Geraldine leaped to her feet. She thought she'd done a rather splendid job of faking the sort of nosy interest someone like Lulu would take in someone else's pregnancy. At least now, when Lulu pumped her mother for Geraldine's response ("But what did she *say*? What were her exact words?") nothing passed on could even hint at a defensive silence. Keeping the act up all evening was going to be a bit more of a trial, but she had made a good start. "I'll fetch your drink."

Robert was waiting in the kitchen. "That's yours. Don't get the two mixed up."

As soon as she tasted it, she realized he had put no gin in with the tonic. He wasn't going to let her get too tipsy to stay on top of things. And she was glad of it the moment she caught sight of Lulu slipping out of her coat in the doorway.

"It seems that Harvey's on his way," Robert announced. "He's busy arguing with some cash machine."

Geraldine hurried over. "Lulu! That bloody warden! He was on the verge of booking me. I must have driven round the block a hundred times. I'm sure Pat saw me waving. I hope she told you, because I did so want to come back in and say congratulations properly. But in the end I just gave up and came on home."

"I must admit that I was worried," Lulu said. "I rather thought, because you didn't ring . . ."

"I *did* ring, Lu. I left about eight messages."

"Really? I didn't get them."

"Odd." Geraldine reached over to the desk and made a bit of a display of rooting round till she unearthed her mobile. Frowning, she pressed the quick dial number they had reprogrammed only half an hour before to one of their deserted laboratories, and then sat waiting.

Nothing rang in the room. "Is yours switched on?" she asked Lulu.

"Mine? Yes."

"Strange, because it's ringing here." She held the phone towards her stepsister. "And now it's taking a message." She spoke into the phone. "Congratulations for the ninth time, Lulu!"

"Tenth," Robert said. "Eleventh, really, if you also count mine." Judging they'd made an adequate stab at being obfuscatory about their failure to be in touch, he turned to his sister-in-law. "Now, Lu, what are you drinking? Water? Orange juice? A virgin Mary? Anything you like."

Back in the kitchen, fetching her fizzy water, he saw a shadow looming on the ribbed glass, and pulled the back door open. Harvey was standing there, staring the other way. "Isn't that your cat on next door's step? Doesn't he know where he lives?"

"I think he sometimes eats there," Robert said. "I expect they use a better brand of cat food."

He waited. And he waited. And then he cracked. "Come *in*," he said, dragging the hapless Harvey inside. "I was just getting your beloved a drink."

"Christ, I could do with one as well," said Harvey. "What an awful day."

"Still," Robert said, "room for congratulations, don't you think?"

For just a moment Harvey looked mystified. Then he caught on. "Oh, that. Oh, yes. Super news, yes."

He sounded about as thrilled as if he'd learned that some troublesome drain outside his door was emptying a tiny bit faster.

"This one will be your third child, won't it?" Robert asked pleasantly.

"Well, actually . . ." said Harvey, and then broke off as though thinking better of sharing the confidence.

To push him into confession, Robert made a guess. "Oh, right! I didn't realize you'd been married before." More to embarrass Harvey than to avoid confusion, he added, "Before, that is, you married *Linda*."

"Well, yes," said Harvey most uneasily. "It just so happens that I was. But we were very young and didn't have kids."

"So, Harvey, are you saying . . .?" It sounded so awful, Robert almost didn't want to suggest it. But it was the only conclusion. "Are you trying to tell me that Linda happens to be pregnant as well?"

Harvey let out a huge sigh. "Christ, Robert. Don't say a thing in there, for my sake! Linda has only just told me tonight. I haven't even had the chance to speak to Lulu."

With what he hoped to be a look of sympathy, Robert passed him a glass. "Knock that back, Harvey. That one's almost neat. Then I'll come back and fill you up again before I lead you into battle."

He stayed to watch poor Harvey wince before piling the other drinks on to a tray and taking them into the living room.

Lulu was on the sofa, her pretty legs stretched in display, already well stuck in to baiting her stepsister. "So there I am, watching that little blue line creep up to hit the bar, and I'm so stupid that I've read all the instructions wrong, and think that means that I'm *not* pregnant. Can you honestly *believe* that?"

"You'd be no good in our lab," Robert told her pleasantly. "Please make a note of that, Geraldine. We must never, ever even consider the idea of hiring your sister." Ceding his usual chair to Harvey, who'd clearly refilled his tumbler to the brim before sidling in behind, he lifted Lulu's legs as casually as if they were some old pile of newspapers, plonked himself down at her side, and dropped the silky long limbs back over his knees. Sitting across from the two of them, Geraldine marvelled. It was a gesture of such brotherly ease that he no longer had to turn to meet Lulu's eye as he asked cheerfully, "So when's it due, this tiny little sprog you've started hatching? Where are we now? March, is it? Will it be here by Christmas as a sort of extra present to the family? I do hope so. Then we'll be able to visit you in a ward full of darling little Noels and little Hollies."

"You just be careful, teasing about names," warned Mrs Carter. "They are a very personal thing indeed, and you can put your foot in it only too easily."

"Somebody in the next-door laboratory to us called their child Bertha last week," Geraldine told them all.

"But things are different these days," Lulu said, "because of all the names from other cultures. You get things like Sasmita and Bikitsha and — what was the name of that gorgeous boy you never got to go out with, Geraldine? Was it Akil?"

Geraldine affected not to have heard. "Oh, Lord! The grill! I clean forgot to turn it off."

She left the room. Shaking his head, Robert rose from the sofa. "While I am letting Geraldine weep on my shoulder about some blackened topping that we must all remember to admire, can I refresh anyone's drink?"

Only poor Harvey passed his glass. Robert went out to the kitchen. "What are you doing?" he asked Geraldine, who was stock still and staring at the clock.

"Sums. I reckon, if they all shove off by twelve, we are .198 of the way through."

"How can you do that so fast without a calculator?"

She stepped aside. He saw the little metal case in front of her on the counter. "Geraldine, put that away and come straight back or they will get suspicious. Especially when they realize that nothing about this supper has been grilled."

"Whoops!"

Obediently, she assumed the calmest of expressions and went back in the room. "All clear! No harm done. Sorry, Lulu. What was that you were saying about deciding to call your baby by some nice, unusual Indian name?"

But they'd moved on, through names to places. Harvey appeared to have laid aside his distraction, and had launched into a tiresome account of how he'd once confused a place called Barnard Castle with Castle Howard. Lulu and Mrs Carter gradually eased themselves out of this conversation, and started on the difference between little girls and little boys. Before abandoning his wife to get on with the last of the cooking, Robert pitched in to steer Harvey on to what they had always found to be his only real topic of conversation. And when he finally called them to take their places at the table, the man was still safely boring on to Geraldine about the various ways in which you could get across the country when certain roads had been closed. "Depends, of course, on just how far away you are when you learn that the snow barriers are down. I mean, if you're on your way south from Newcastle on the A1 —"

"You sit here, Jane. You're not in any draught from the kitchen, I hope?"

"No, no. I'm fine."

"— then there is not much you can do. But just north of Penrith on the M6, as you come past —"

"And Lulu, you're sitting here."

"Lovely."

"Travelling up from the south it's quite a different matter. There is the M18, of course, but after that —"

"Harvey. Sit here, please."

He took his place, still grinding on about alternative ways to cross the Pennines. It took the social skills of Robert's mother-in-law to stem the tide. "Harvey, you seem to have done a very great deal of travelling in your life. But where were you brought up? And what was your first job?"

Bugger, thought Robert. Now Jane is going to stare into his eyes and let him bore her for the general good while, at our end of the table, Lulu goes on the rampage.

She did, too. Barely a moment passed before she got started. He had the feeling Lulu didn't even know that she was doing it. "This all looks nice," she said, staring down at the shining knives and forks and pretty side plates. "Some people are really, really good at entertaining, aren't they? I have some friends in London, and they're *amazing*. They get you round and make you feel so welcome. The food's delicious. Absolutely delicious. It keeps on coming. They're generous with the drinks, too. And they choose *such* nice wine. You really ought to meet them."

"We really must," said Robert. He didn't add the rider, "Might pick up some tips," because he had seen Geraldine's forced smile and felt her touch on his thigh. Instead, he leaned across, holding out one of the bottles. "White, Lulu? Or would you prefer red? Oh, sorry. Of course, I had forgotten. You *can't*."

But that was as far as he dared go, through all Lulu's little stabbings. "You know the sort of woman. Wears tweed skirts. Oh! I don't mean like that one you wear so often, Geraldine. I mean the ones that make even *normal* people look stout . . . No, honestly. It was the longest evening I have ever suffered. First they insisted that we all went out to look at their flowers. I mean, what *is* it with people who spend their whole lives gardening? I know you two seem practically to *live* up at the garden centre. But even you can't be *that* obsessed . . ." On it went, on and on. Thank God he was left-handed, so it seemed natural to set his glass down on the table beside his wife's. He made great play of topping up both of the glasses each time, but was discreet about the fact that he was the only one ever to drink from either.

Finally, *finally*, the plates were cleared. "I'll sort them out," said Robert. But Geraldine was off the mark at once. "No, no. You know the rules." Since neither of them wanted a shift in their usual household patterns to set the cogs in Lulu's brain turning, he didn't argue. He knew that Lulu would follow her stepsister through as usual, to slip in a few more demoralizing remarks while she pretended to give a hand. But Geraldine had to be stone-cold sober. She could maintain her streak of steel.

Geraldine glanced at the clock as she flicked on the taps. If they left shortly, say not much later than half past, then almost six-sevenths of the evening was safely gone. Stay cool. Stay calm. Here came the footfalls already.

The minute she walked through the door, Lulu was on her case. "Geraldine! I'm so glad for this chance to have a word. I mean, I'm really worried that this business of me being pregnant is going to be hard on Robert."

The shock was huge. It was as much as Geraldine could manage to bite back the wail of pain. Forcing herself not to cry out, "On Robert? Why on *Robert*?", she gripped the side of the sink. "Oh, Lulu! That is so *sweet* of you to worry about him." Fearing her whitening knuckles would give her away, she let go and turned. "*And* about me, I'm sure. But, honestly, you *mustn't.* We are both terribly embarrassed we wasted so much money on those two consultations. But, truly, we can look at other people's babies without having to blush about our sheer stupidity."

Command performance! Thank God that she and Robert had not just worked out exactly the line to take, they'd almost practised. Turning back to the sink, she stuck an arm out sideways and said casually, "Pass me those dishes, there's an angel. I'll drop them in to soak." Without giving Lulu any chance to interrupt, she pressed on with the story they'd concocted. "I mean, of course I do still feel a wally. I should have *guessed* that Robert was only lying to me about wanting a baby because he assumed I was keen. And I was only lying through my teeth to him because I was convinced he had once said he wanted a large family. But, as that clinic advisor kept on telling us, it wasn't *such* a dreadful waste of time and money because, once they had taken us into separate counselling sessions, they did at least manage to prise the truth out of us both."

She turned to smile at Lulu. "You can *imagine* just what fools we felt when we were brought together afterwards. I could have died! But it was worth it when you think about it. After all, the whole embarrassing business can only have added up to a mere fraction of what it costs to go on by mistake and have a baby."

She glanced sideways at Lulu. "And you will be all right, that way, won't you?"

It was as if Lulu wasn't quite keeping up to speed. "What? Do you mean with money?"

"Yes. Because, you know, children are *horribly* expensive." Hastily Geraldine brushed her own question aside. "But it's so wonderful — for *all* of us, not just for you and Harvey. I mean, we get the joy of having a baby in the family. Mum must be over the moon. I know that she's been hoping for years that one of us would crack."

Turning from the sink, Geraldine took Lulu by the shoulders, looked in her eyes, and then, with the warmest of smiles, she hugged her tight. "And now you've done it, Lulu! Oh, well done! Well done!"

CHAPTER
FIVE

They were astonished at the dizzying pace at which Harvey's wife appeared to go at the divorce. "My God!" said Robert, putting down the phone after Lulu had yet again brought them up to date. "That Linda doesn't hang about. She must be desperate to be rid of the man. How long did that lab technician of yours — what was his name —?"

"Howard."

"How long did it take Howard to get his marriage bust-up sorted out?"

"Years. Absolutely years. But then, his wife was stalling all along the way, pretending she hadn't got letters, refusing to fill in forms, and arguing right up to the last minute about money and arrangements for the children."

"That's the odd bit," said Robert. "You'd think, especially with being pregnant again, this Linda would have hunkered down and hoped that Harvey would think better of the whole business."

"Perhaps she isn't pregnant any more."

"That's possible." Gently he steered away from one more topic that he knew made Geraldine unhappy — how deeply unfair it was that so many women could pick and choose between the options that were closed to others. "Well, that's one question we can't ask . . ."

"No," she said firmly. "We can't."

He shook his head. To him, it seemed pretty well out of the question that Harvey might not have passed on to Lulu the news that his wife was pregnant too — indeed, after all that gin, might even have forgotten that he'd told Robert. But Geraldine was less convinced. "He's such a head-in-the-sand bungler. I wouldn't be at all surprised if Lulu knows nothing about it."

"And she can be such a secretive little madam. *I* wouldn't be surprised if she has known from the start, and simply hasn't told us."

Pushing Puffer aside, he threw himself down and switched on the television. Covertly Geraldine watched him. There was something so different about the way he had begun to talk of Lulu. Beneath the old amusement and contempt now lay true anger. More and more over the last few weeks, Geraldine had had the feeling that her husband was cruising near a kind of hate for someone he had only bothered to despise before. Look at him now, sprawled on the sofa gnawing at a hangnail. He didn't have the usual bland expression of someone half-absorbed in Saturday's match.

She reached down behind the cushions till her fingers closed around the zapper. In less than a moment she had blanked out the screen. "Test question! Who was playing who?"

"Tottenham against Blackburn."

She moved away so she could switch the screen back on before he grabbed back the zapper. The little letters at the top were clear enough.

"Liar. It's Arsenal and someone called WHU."

"West Ham United," he said automatically, then added coldly, "And your *point*?"

Switching the television off for good, she sat beside him. "Robert, what is the *matter*? I know that we decided not to let Lulu know she'd rattled our cage. But it's as if there's something more to it for you now. You seem so utterly pissed off with her."

Uneasily, he shifted away. She moved up close. He pulled away again. Making a joke of it, she bounced herself along. He didn't smile, but she persisted.

"Robert —"

He glowered at her and his face went red. Then out it burst. "I am!" he said. "I really am."

"What?"

"Pissed off with Lulu." Even to him it sounded childish. "At first I thought that I was just exasperated, as usual. When this began, I thought I was mad at her because, as ever, she was being so vilely careless with other people's feelings." He took her hand. "Especially yours. But every day I loathe her more." Seeing her look of astonishment, he drew his fingers back as if he feared the contact might contaminate his wife. "Yes, Geraldine. I truly, truly loathe her. I loathe her for every messy, stupid decision that she makes."

"It's only one decision. Well, two really."

He jumped to his feet. "It *isn't* only two. Each of the stupid things she does spawns twenty more daft things that will cause pain to others. And it's so *unnecessary*. If Lulu stopped to think for even a moment, she couldn't do what she does."

The sheer force of his feeling made her lean over backwards to be fair to the stepsister she knew so well. "Anyone can fall in love."

He snorted. "Not this blindly. Not grown people. Harvey is such an obvious shit, and such an obvious wanker, she doesn't even have to stop and think."

And that was true enough. They both fell silent, thinking about Harvey. The problem was, the man was so dull and weak and bland that it was easy to forget that no one with a shred of decency could ever act the way he did.

"Certainly the man's idea of marriage is a farce. In, out, in, out."

"If we could only find out more about his job I'd feel a little happier."

Lord knows, they'd tried. When he was cornered, Harvey talked civilly enough about a meeting in Leeds here, an exhibition in Tatton Park there, a recent tiresome journey. But though the two of them had both as good as asked him, "But what is it exactly that you *do*?", the answers that he offered were somehow so flabby and opaque that Robert was convinced he was in sales and marketing while Geraldine had gradually formed the opinion that advertising was his game.

"I don't know why we're worrying about bloody Lulu."

"Neither do I." She couldn't help it, though. Geraldine might be immersed in an unspoken feud with her foul stepsister. But family — however stretched the term — still kept its grip. You couldn't blithely leave any of them to fall in the gutter — if only for fear of having to spend more effort later, when you had finally cracked, pulling them out again. In any case, the baby that was coming had played no part in getting into the mess. Poor bloody mite. How could they walk away from that?

She tried to cheer herself. "Maybe things aren't as bad as we imagine. Perhaps, even after the divorce, there will still be enough left over for him and Lulu. After all, he might be a whole lot more successful at making money than we suspect."

He was still scowling. "Harvey? Only if his job is gun-running. Or smuggling drugs. Or importing Eastern European girls to work in sex clubs. Fat chance!" He realized what he'd said. "What I mean is —"

"I know what you mean. You would feel happier if you were sure that somewhere — even in his choice of job — the man had some sort of spine." She sighed. "Oh, God. Poor Lulu."

Again the fury coiled inside him stirred. "Poor Lulu, nothing! She's bringing the whole damn boiling down on herself, indulging herself this way. Be honest, Geraldine. If you had fallen for someone and it became clear not only that he'd failed at his first marriage, but that his second wife couldn't get rid of him fast enough — can't *wait* to agree to any old arrangement and sign the papers — wouldn't that make you wonder?" He didn't wait for her response. "Of course it would! So bugger 'poor Lulu'. Poor twins is what I say. And, now, poor baby."

"Poor *babies*," Geraldine corrected him. "And we don't *know*. Perhaps this Linda is glad the marriage is coming to an end, for all she's pregnant. And maybe she and Harvey have managed to come to a fair and sensible deal."

"Perhaps they have. In which case, he is married to a gem and should think twice before he walks out on her. *And* on his kids." He shook a finger at his wife. "No, Geraldine, don't try to let Lulu wriggle off the hook on this one. Here she goes, mucking up more lives with her complete and utter selfishness." He threw himself back against the sofa. "She is so *messy*."

There was a long, long silence. Then Robert lifted his head. "Do you remember, back in school, when you had to learn that poem?"

"What poem?"

"The one for smoking in the changing rooms. By that bloke in the bin."

"County Asylum."

"Whatever. Well, there was something in that about messy women."

Nobody ever forgot a punishment poem, because for every error that you made reciting it, you had to copy it out another time.

"*I long for scenes where man has never trod,*" she said. "*For scenes where woman never smiled nor wept.*"

"Yes, that's the one." He scowled. "It didn't mean a thing back then, when I was testing you. But, by Christ,

I understand it now. That's how I feel about *her*. I wish the bloody woman never smiled nor wept because every tiny damn thing she does never fails to cause trouble for others."

She inched a little closer. "You don't think, because of this baby business, the two of us might have become a little obsessed?"

"You mean me, don't you?"

She took his hand. "Come on, now. I said both of us."

"But you mean me."

"No. I agreed to that mad plan to smile at everything she does. Perhaps we should change tack. You could try heading her off whenever she starts going on about being pregnant in front of me. And I could tell her that you are disgusted at what will happen to those poor twins."

"Shall we?"

"Why not?"

"It's very tempting, isn't it? I wonder what she'd do."

"Sulk? Stay away?"

They sat together quietly. But they knew Lulu all too well. Robert said finally, "She will just crow it over us, won't she?"

And Geraldine agreed. "She will just crow."

CHAPTER
SIX

It sounded so horribly calculating. But if they skipped another week before making contact, Lulu might start to think they were avoiding her. Then all the efforts they had made so far to seem entirely unperturbed would come to nothing. Robert was clearly still in the darkest of moods about his sister-in-law. So taking advantage of the only day of the week in which she and her husband travelled to the laboratories in separate cars, Geraldine waited till Robert had set off for home, then hastily packed up her own work and drove off towards the perpetually deserted gift shop in which her stepsister now worked three days a week.

It was an easier trip than she expected around the bypass, and shortly before five thirty she was letting the rainbow-painted door swing closed behind her. "You're still open, then?"

"Till eight," said Lulu, looking up from a heap of glossy swimsuits she was removing from their plastic hangers.

Not liking to admit she'd meant the shop itself, not just the hours, Geraldine told her, "Say if you're busy. I don't want to interrupt."

"No, no. It's good to see you. It's been horribly quiet all day. And I feel crap."

Geraldine made the usual effort. "You poor thing! Are you nauseous?"

"A little, yes. Bloated and headachy."

"At least you *look* fantastic."

"I am blooming, aren't I?" As though to prove it, Lulu cleared a space on the counter, then turned and hitched herself up. It was the neatest move, discountenancing Geraldine both by its sheer agility and grace, and by the beauty of the legs displayed to such effect as, lazily, her stepsister crossed one knee over the other. "So. Are you on the prowl?"

"On the prowl?"

"For a gift." Lulu waved a manicured hand. "We have some brand-new china stuff over there, and there are a few unusual scarves in that big basket. Or are you after some sort of treat for yourself?" Reaching behind her, she picked up one of the swimsuits. "How about trying on one of these?"

It would, thought Geraldine, be a rare day on which she ever volunteered to expose her body's ineradicable plumpness to Lulu again. Still, out of politeness she reached for the gleaming, ruched affair. "How can a gift shop like this sell swimsuits?"

"We can't." Lulu grinned. "At least, *I* can't. Tara's sold three or four and thinks they're definitely the way to go. But I've not managed to shift a single one."

Not a surprise. Which of the shoppers who ended up in here could withstand Lulu's smirk as they went off behind the curtain to squeeze their chubby bottoms and dimpled thighs into these unforgiving garments? Who'd have the nerve to call, "Can I try the next size up?" or dare come out to face that "I-am-saying-nothing" look? No. All the customers would just despair. They'd shove the swimsuits back on the rack, hurriedly muttering, "Not sure the colour suits me," and flee from the utterly lovely Lulu, who was still managing to look as if, were she to sneeze, her silky bodice would slither with a whisper to the floor. What did they do in bed, Harvey and Lulu? It was quite clear to Geraldine why, always before, Harvey should have kept feeling the urge to return to his wife and family. But what were the sexual wiles that had made him — and all the others — run back to Lulu time and again, even when they were well aware of her insufferable character?

"Geraldine, you can't want that!"

Startled, she looked down at the painted plate she had picked up to cover her wild imaginings. "I thought the cat looked rather cute."

"Oh, put it down."

Obediently, Geraldine laid the ghastly thing back on its wire stand. "So how are things with Harvey?"

"Fine."

"You're neither of you finding it a little difficult to share the flat?"

"Not in the slightest. I think the two of us were made for one another."

Too right, thought Geraldine. Like matches and straw. "Any plans for the weekend?"

"We're going down to friends."

She felt obliged to ask, "His friends, or yours?" although she guessed the answer. Lulu had very few friends — at least, few of the sort in a position to offer hospitality through whole weekends. Her sort of troublemaking soon put a stop to most of her relationships with steady couples. Only the truly lonely were prepared to trade their empty hours for Lulu's habitual scratching at their self-image. What was it she had said to Eleanor Hodge about her husband? "He has a dozen ways of being dreary, doesn't he?" When Stephanie told her that Tom had finally suggested the two of them move in together, Lulu had said, "He must be a whole lot lonelier than we thought." And when that sweet little couple, John and Jennie Tanner, showed her with such pride round their first London flat, she had apparently announced, "Well, I suppose that people can be happy *anywhere*."

So. His friends, then. And so it proved.

"They're mates of Harvey's, somewhere down in Kent. I've not met them before."

She looked quite pleased at the idea of going — as well she might, thought Geraldine, since even if she didn't choose to relish any of the usual pleasures of the countryside, her hosts would surely furnish her with two fresh targets for her hobby: spite.

"Taking a gift?" asked Geraldine, waving an arm at all the stuff set out so artfully on tables and shelves.

"Christ, no!" said Lulu. "You wouldn't catch me dead in here buying any of this crap."

And there it was, that horribly unstoppable rush of blood to Geraldine's cheeks. On Lulu's face shone the familiar smile that meant, "One up to me." Now there was no way Geraldine could try to claim she'd just come in the shop to say hello. The words would sound as lame and unconvincing as when a child says, "I didn't want it anyway," when someone snatches away her toy.

"Actually, I was looking for something for Mum."

"Really?" Lulu made a face. "Is she still down in the dumps?"

News to her daughter. But Geraldine would not admit to Lulu that she knew more than others in the family about Jane Carter's frame of mind. So she just hedged. "Oh, I don't know. I can't really make it out. But still, I thought I might go round there and take something nice."

"Take something to eat, then."

"Something to eat?"

"Yes." Lulu made a face. "You'd be a whole lot safer, that's for sure. When she had Harvey and me round on Tuesday night —"

"Tuesday?"

Lulu pressed on as if she hadn't heard. "— she offered us what must have been the worst meal ever." Lulu was grinning now. "I thought she must have been crying into it all day, but Harvey was convinced she'd added washing-up liquid to the sauce."

Geraldine knew she ought to leave it. Ask her mother later. It was another Lulu trap. And yet she couldn't help it. "But Tuesday is her bridge night."

"Yes." Lulu's face beamed innocence. "But Jane just skipped it."

Deeper and deeper into the hole she went. "Really? Missed bridge?"

Lulu shrugged. "It was the easiest evening for us."

No point in even trying to hide the look of hurt. The damage was already done. She had *invited* it. Still, Geraldine turned away. What *was* it about the way her mother so often favoured Lulu? Jane Carter and her bridge partner, Anna, pretty much lived to beat the Edelfords on Tuesday nights. ("They're just so *snotty*, Geraldine. If things don't go their way, they have the nerve to look astonished. And even when they're winning, they have this truly annoying way of acting as if everything's doing no more than fall out as it should.") How many times had Geraldine suggested a film or play, and had the offer refused before she finally realized her mother's Tuesday schedule was set in stone? Yet here was Lulu, who had no responsibilities and no real schedule, and suddenly the habit of years had been shelved to indulge her. It was *infuriating*. She had been stupid to come. By now she could have been at home and halfway through her second cup of tea — perhaps even making a dent in this year's trainee application forms. And what was she doing instead? Biting her tongue at Lulu's sneering remarks, making herself miserable by letting herself be reminded of just how often her mother put herself out for Lulu more than she did for her own daughter; and feeling horrid at the thought of how this ungrateful pair were sniggering about Jane's lack of cooking skills behind her back. Robert was right. Every damn thing to do with Lulu led

56

to hurt or disquiet, and she'd been mad to step inside the shop.

"So," she said, turning back with a bright smile, "I make the effort to find a parking space and walk down here to get advice on what might cheer Mum up, and you say that there's nothing in the shop to do the trick."

"No," Lulu said. "Nothing to sort out what is wrong with her. The only thing that would do that is you deciding to get pregnant too."

Oh, Christ! How did she do it? How did this stuff keep spilling out of her? Just like that girl in the fairy tale, Lulu could spit *toads*. And how could Geraldine disguise her gasp of pain? Quick! Reach for the ugliest thing in sight!

She picked it up. A ghastly painted terracotta biscuit barrel in the shape of a duck. "This is quite something."

"Isn't it?"

Forcing her hands to stop shaking, Geraldine put the duck down carefully on the counter. Lulu stared at the ghastly yellow monstrosity. "You surely don't want to buy this?"

"Yes, I do."

"Not for Jane, surely."

"No, no. Someone else." She couldn't for the life of her think fast enough, so heard herself adding inanely, "I think it's perfect for my purposes."

Lulu, of course, would not give up. "Which are?"

Some sort of answer finally came to Geraldine. "It's for a teenager. This lad who worked in our lab. He's off to university and I think it'll be useful. All students stuff themselves with biscuits, and this will be a talking point in his college room."

"The end of his social life, I'd have thought," Lulu said sourly. Still, she reached out to slide a few sheets of the rainbow-coloured tissue paper off her thick pile, and carefully began to wrap the lurid terracotta duck. "What about Jane?"

Geraldine took a grip of herself and said as bravely as she could, "Well, I'm afraid she's on a hiding to nothing if what she wants is a baby from me."

"Actually, I meant the *gift*."

She couldn't lift her eyes again to meet that "gotcha!" smile. So Geraldine stared at the floor while Lulu spread the bubble wrap across the counter. Dear gods, it was like going five rounds in a prize fight. There must be something she could think of to deflect Lulu's next lunge. Work? Weather? Holiday plans?

Lulu was faster, of course. "I expect that you're hoping one baby will be enough for Jane, aren't you? I mean, what with all that you were saying a while ago about neither of you being keen." Skilfully, she slid the ungainly padded shape into one of the shop's sleek cardboard carriers and lifted her eyes to peer into Geraldine's face. "Well, you'll be lucky! Because you know you've always been the favourite."

"I'm not sure —"

"Oh, don't be daft. Of *course* you are. You're her *real* daughter, after all. I am just someone she as good as picked up off the street."

"Lulu —"

58

But now her stepsister was on a roll. "You've always been *far* more important than I have. It's what *you* do that matters, not what I do."

Geraldine was too wiped out even to try to keep her end up. "Lulu, what are you on about?"

"Nothing." Back came the innocent look. "I was just trying to explain that it's not surprising that my getting pregnant has set Jane off again, thinking about what she's missing, not getting any grandchild from you. I'm not surprised that she's down in the dumps."

She slid the carrier across the counter, and made one of her rare attempts at joking. "So, ma'am, will that be all?"

"Oh, yes," said Geraldine, squeezing out a smile. And it took all her force of will not to add bitterly, "Oh, yes. I think that's quite enough."

CHAPTER
SEVEN

She phoned home from the car park. Robert picked up on the first ring. "Where are you? I was expecting you home nearly an hour ago. Are you all right?"

"Of course I'm all right. I've just been having a little chat with Lulu."

"She rang you?"

"Yes." For heaven's sake, why lie to *him*? "Well, actually, no. To be honest, I suddenly took it into my head to stop off at the shop on the way home."

"More fool you. And . . .?"

"And Lulu says that Mum is very much down in the dumps."

There was a pause, and then he said, "I doubt that, Geraldine."

"What do you mean?"

"Just that it would be odd. Your mother doesn't really have moods, does she?"

"Everyone has moods."

"Not everyone. Not her."

It was a strange idea but, pushing it aside, Geraldine pressed on. "Well, I just thought I might go round there for a cup of tea and see what's going on."

"There won't be anything going on. All it'll be is Lulu needling you."

Geraldine sighed. "She's already managed that. I'll tell you later." She took advantage of the poor reception to end the call. "Don't hold off supper if you're starving."

"I'll be all right. Puffer and I can snack on liver chunks."

"Oh, please!" She slid the phone back in her bag and got in the car. Was it true, what he had claimed, that Jane did not have moods? Geraldine thought back. Certainly her mother seemed to have a steady nature. Geraldine had no real memories of floods of tears, or bouts of anger, either before or during the divorce. And things were calm enough after. Experience and self-control can be hard-won, though. What about when Jane Carter was younger, before she found herself saddled with the responsibility of keeping up a more or less unruffled front in front of her small daughter? When she had run away with Esteban she'd been a bit of a hippie, so she claimed. And certain aspects of that way of life had certainly stuck. Jane Carter rarely bothered to replace things that weren't yet broken. She never had to get herself into the habit of recycling things like garden waste and glass and paper because she'd never stopped. She seemed quite settled in herself as well. Geraldine had never heard her fret about her greying hair and deepening wrinkles. She was quite calm about emergencies. She didn't get annoyed about things that she read in the papers.

Perhaps Robert was right. But that meant either Lulu was inventing nonsense or, just this once, something had touched her mother deeply. Could it be true, as Lulu claimed, that Geraldine was the only one who really mattered, and Jane's distress stemmed from the fact that it was Lulu who was going to have a baby, while Geraldine had more or less announced she'd never follow in her wake?

It all seemed so *unlikely*. But Geraldine had now lost confidence in her own judgement. It almost came as a relief when she was forced to concentrate on the horrendous traffic. And it was not till she peeled off down the side streets towards her mother's pretty block of maisonettes that she could even try to think the whole peculiar business through again. This time, she tried to come at things in a more robust fashion. Surely she couldn't have been wrong all of her life about her mother's feelings. It was too hard to believe that all that leaning over backwards to assuage Lulu had been no more than an attempt to disguise the fact that, at heart, she preferred her own daughter. What about all those times when Lulu's petty desires had come before Geraldine's real needs? The night before her music exam, when they'd all had to stay in the city until late just because Lulu made such a fuss about seeing that film about bears. The cancellation of Geraldine's school trip to France just so that she would be around to "help Lulu feel a little more at home" in her first couple of weeks back in their house after Jed died. Even the way that Lulu always seemed to get first pick at everything — "I'll have the red one, please!", "Bagsie the bed by the window!" — till what had started as a way of trying to cheer up, first, a brand-new stepchild, and, second time around, a teenager who'd lost her father, had turned into a habit Jane Carter made no effort to break.

No, no. The whole idea was nonsense. How could so many deeply hurtful moments take place because of some sham front thrown up to hide a deeper love?

Her mother's car was in its numbered spot. Geraldine fished inside the dashboard pocket to find the permit she'd not used for quite a while. *Guest of 8B.* And that, she realized somewhat ruefully, is what she felt like. Slightly detached. More guest than daughter — actually, on this occasion, more social worker than guest.

She took the long route round the flowerbeds for fear of meeting up with any of the other residents on the shortcut through the bushes. Last time she'd come, she'd felt obliged to carry some old biddy's shopping bags right the way over the complex, then help her unpack. She hadn't time for that sort of thing today. It would be good to get in and assure herself that Lulu was just making waves as usual. Then she could slide off home — to Robert, who would no doubt lift her spirits by joking that the only mood Jane Carter could have been suffering from on Tuesday night would have been irritation at having let smart little Lulu outmanoeuvre her into missing her precious bridge night.

Her mother looked cheery enough as she answered the door. "Geraldine! What a great treat! I have been thinking all day that it would be nice to ring for a chat. I was just waiting till you'd had time to get home and unwind. What's brought you round my way?"

"Just suddenly took it into my head to surprise you."

"I'm glad you did."

While her mother was grinding the coffee beans, Geraldine looked around. There was no sign that anything was amiss. The flowers were fresh in their vase. The magazines were tidy on the table. Her mother had obviously put down a book to answer the door. The kitchen was as spruce as usual.

"Just using your loo."

"Fine, dear."

Geraldine coughed to cover the tell-tale click as she tugged at the medicine-cabinet door. Behind the mirror there were no surprises, only the usual buffered aspirin and vitamins, the herbal sleeping pills her mother swore by in spite of Robert's active scorn, corn plasters, hair grips, a few old medicines. Nothing that could have been prescribed since Geraldine last peeked.

Pushing the mirror back just as the cistern reached the noisiest part of its cycle, she came back out. "You're looking very good," she told her mother.

"Am I? Well, why not?"

"Have you been busy?"

"I suppose that things are much the same as usual."

Geraldine wondered whether or not to pursue it. She could, for example, innocently ask, "So how did you and Anna fare on Tuesday? Pounded the snotty Edelfords into the dust, I hope." But Lulu was more than mischievous enough to mention the conversation that had taken place. And then it would be obvious that, far from popping in on a spontaneous visit, Geraldine had been as good as checking up on what her mother told her about the details of her life — and what she didn't.

Safer by far not to act disingenuous. "I just called in on Lulu at the shop."

"She's all right, isn't she? No problems?"

"Not that she said. In fact, she looked amazing. She said that she was nauseous, but it didn't seem to be bothering her." Geraldine studied her mother's face. "You're surely not worried, are you? You haven't noticed anything wrong?"

"Me? No."

"No food fads?" Geraldine persisted.

"Well, dear, I wouldn't know about that." But Geraldine had sensed a hesitation, as if her mother suddenly thought better of coming out with something else. Now what might that have been? Perhaps a little lie along the lines of, "I've barely seen her, actually"? Or maybe even the plain truth: "Though they did happen to come round here on Tuesday night."

Nothing. In silence Geraldine's mother leaned forward to push the awkward little plunger down the glass jug. Geraldine felt she had stepped too far into the conversation not to come clean, so she asked openly, "How was she when the two of them came round for supper?"

She couldn't work out from her mother's face if she was startled. Certainly Jane Carter's response sounded straightforward enough. "She was in quite a good mood. She did complain a little about feeling queasy. But she admitted even that was getting better by the day."

"And Harvey? In good spirits?"

"When isn't he?"

Geraldine sighed. "It's quite amazing, isn't it? I mean, here they are, thrown into this situation, a baby on its way, and Harvey simply bats along as if there's nothing on earth to worry about and everything will come out right."

And there it was, that slightly weary look upon her mother's face, as if Jane Carter were thinking: Oh, here we go.

She kept her voice light, though. "And you think it might not?"

Geraldine didn't see why, just because her mother preferred the role of ostrich, she herself should be forced to play it as well. "I'm not sure that it will. He's being rather optimistic, isn't he? I realize that, so far, his wife has been almost miraculously easy-going. But who's to say that's going to last?"

"It certainly sounds as if this Linda's happy enough to be rid of him."

It was her mother's casual tone that startled Geraldine. She spoke as if she were remarking on nothing more significant than someone getting rid of a garden shed. Maybe it was this business of watching others being so cavalier with a great privilege you'd never have yourself, but Geraldine had to speak out. "Well, there's a problem right there. What if this Linda thinks the little boys ought to be happy to be rid of him too? That attitude's common enough."

"Yes," Mrs Carter admitted. "But it is also quite common for men like Harvey not to mind too much."

Strange to think this observation had been put forward as a positive. The very notion irritated Geraldine. "I suppose so. After all, no one is going to rush to offer Harvey any medals for making efforts to be responsible."

And there it was again: that little frown. "Aren't you being just the tiniest bit unfair?"

Oh, really!

It had been a singularly draining couple of hours. She'd made enough mistakes in opening her mouth already, Geraldine reckoned. So why not make one more? "Come off it, Mum. Look at his track record! He has been cheating on Linda pretty well since the day he married her."

Jane Carter looked shocked. "What, all that time? With Lulu?"

"Who else?"

"I don't think that I knew that, dear."

It was the sort of wilful self-deception her daughter found hardest to bear. Trying her best not to sound too accusing, Geraldine reminded her, "Oh, yes, I think you did. We all did. In fact, I clearly remember you disapproving of one of Robert's jokes about the fact that, if his new wife found out that Harvey was sleeping with someone else already, she was probably within her rights to go for an annulment rather than a divorce."

"He went back very quickly though, that time."

So she remembered that bit clearly enough. And that, of course, was always the way her mother dealt with everything to do with Lulu. She kept a firm grip on the things about her life that didn't cause vexation or misery, and airbrushed all the others out. But Geraldine was irritated enough at this reminder of her mother's capacity to be selective about what she chose to notice and recall, to respond tartly, "Harvey has gone back very quickly *every* time."

"Oh, dear." As if her daughter's remark had knocked some of the stuffing out of her, Mrs Carter sank back against the cushions. "So you don't think that Harvey and Lulu are going to last?"

"I didn't say that. How should I know what's going to happen?"

"You're not confident, though."

Geraldine sighed. "How can I be?" She wondered if this might be the moment to ask her mother if she realized that Linda was pregnant as well. But she and Robert still didn't know if Lulu had been told. Such news might easily filter back and it could not be right to shock a pregnant woman in that way.

Then again, maybe it wasn't right to let Lulu sail on through her pregnancy not knowing something so significant. Her stepsister might prefer to think again about her future with Harvey.

"Mum, how pregnant *is* Lulu?"

"I'm really not at all sure, dear. She's a bit cagey with me."

"And me."

"Perhaps she doesn't want anyone trying to be too *sensible* about it," suggested Mrs Carter. "You know. Giving advice she doesn't want to hear."

"Do you mean telling her she ought to think of getting rid of it?"

"Perhaps."

"Do you mean *me*?"

The tone was vague. "Not you especially, dear."

Geraldine fought back. "Well, I know better than to suggest anything on earth to Lulu. She goes her own way. But I must say that if Harvey were the father of any baby of mine, I'd certainly think twice."

"That sounds a little harsh."

"No. Just realistic. You're surely not going to try to pretend you don't have anxieties yourself. Harvey is hardly the steady sort. I mean, the man just chops and changes. He can't stick at anything. And neither can she. Who would be mad enough to prophesy a steady and successful relationship?"

"Oh, Geraldine! You really are worrying me."

Geraldine stared. Was that a *criticism*? Yes, it was. Her mother actually had the nerve to look reproachful, as if she thought her daughter was coming out with all these remarks simply to be upsetting. Clearly she would prefer to be allowed to stay in some dream world in which it was perfectly reasonable to assume that things for Lulu and Harvey were halfway to hunky-dory now, and very possibly might stay that way for ever. For the first time in her life, Geraldine could almost imagine her mother at one of those old hippy festivals from years ago. Was this the sort of sloppy, hopeful thinking that had been all around her in those days? Wipe away the wrinkles, put her in a flapping flowered skirt, and Geraldine could almost see her mother taking on that spaced-out, vacant look that she herself had always associated with people who prefer soft drugs to hard, hard facts.

She wasn't going to take the blame for any of her mother's unease. "It's not *me* worrying you. It's the situation."

"You do seem rather determined that things are bound to go wrong."

"That's not quite fair!"

"I'm sorry, dear. I suppose all I meant to say is that not everybody's relationship is quite like yours and Robert's. Harvey is quite mercurial, I agree —"

"*Mercurial?*"

Mrs Carter spoke almost sharply. "Yes, that's right. Mercurial. And Lulu, as we know, is pretty up and down herself. But that's not to say they can't make things work out nicely between them."

"How? I should be very surprised if Harvey earns enough to keep two families. And Lulu earns peanuts, and probably won't be earning anything at all within a very short time. And she's a spender."

"Money's not everything."

"Linda's not going to let her own children go short because of Lulu's baby."

"We don't know anything at all about that side of things. It's not for us to try to guess the state of affairs between Harvey and his ex-wife."

"She isn't ex yet."

"She will be very soon. And people who fail at one relationship can often succeed perfectly well at another. So I think, rather than revelling in some great black cloud of doubt over their future —"

"That's not what I was doing!"

"— we ought to try to be happy for them, and wish them well."

Her mother finished this short speech by quite deliberately looking down and pretending to pick at flaws in her fingernail polish, while Geraldine sat quietly, feeling like a scolded child. She'd no idea why Lulu had suggested her mother's spirits had seemed low. To Geraldine, she seemed more than usually gung-ho.

Hostile, in fact.

Best to bail out before they quarrelled properly.

"Is that the time? I suppose I really ought to be getting back. I promised Robert I'd be home for supper." Out of politeness, she asked her mother, "You wouldn't like to join us, would you? You'd be most welcome. I could drive you home."

"No, no. I've something sorted."

"Righty-ho." Geraldine lifted her jacket off the chair by the door. She felt uneasy. On an impulse, she turned back. "You won't pass any of this conversation back to Lulu, will you? They're just between the two of us, these doubts of mine. The day that Lulu marries, I do want to be able to stand there smiling like everyone else, popping champagne corks. I wouldn't want a damper putting on her day because she knew that I had doubts."

Jane Carter softened enough to smile. She came across to pat her worried daughter's hand. "Oh, Geraldine, I know you're only being honest. And I do understand."

They hugged. But on her way back to the car, Geraldine felt strangely disquieted. Wondering what was the matter, she realized the tension in her stomach had barely lessened. And what was unnerving her so much was that, in spite of her mother's last words of reassurance, the feeling of unease had not yet fully gone.

CHAPTER
EIGHT

" 'Mercurial'! Is that what she called Harvey? By god, your mother has a whitewash brush the size of Kent."

"When she chooses to use it." Geraldine busied herself reaching down plates from the cabinets. But once the table was set and she was sitting across from him, fork in hand, she asked, seemingly out of the blue, "Robert, where do you think I came from?"

"Sorry?"

"I don't mean *now*. Character-wise, I mean. I can't take after my father, can I? He was a Spanish hippy. And though Mum leads a steady enough life these days — bridge evenings and all — you only have to look at her track record to see a few rough bumps. So where on earth did someone like me come from?"

"You know it doesn't work like that."

"I know Mum wishes it did." She pushed the pepper mill that he was reaching for closer towards him. "Honestly, Robert, you should have heard her tonight. She couldn't stick up for that flaky pair enough. It wasn't just her calling Harvey 'mercurial'. She was just as defensive about Lulu. 'A little up and down,' she called her."

Robert grinned. "Certainly up and down enough to make some people nauseous."

But Geraldine didn't respond. She sat absorbed in her own thoughts. Suddenly sensing trouble, he reached behind him for the roll of kitchen paper. While she was staring at her plate, he ripped a few sheets off in readiness.

Finally she spoke. "Actually, it was worse than that. Far worse. In fact, it was rather horrible. I got the feeling Mum was sitting there, halfway to disliking me. I'm sure she didn't mean to give her feelings away, but there was something about the way things went that made it rather obvious she thought I was repellent."

"Oh, really, Geraldine!"

"No, hear me out. I'm not imagining it. I'm not exaggerating, either. It started really early on, so I was careful. I only said a tiny bit of what was true about the situation, and still she made me feel so moralistic and so negative." Geraldine put down her fork and stared at Robert blankly across the table. "Actually, I don't believe my mother likes me very much."

Robert reached out to tug her plate closer towards his own. "You mustn't cry in the carpaccio," he warned her gently. "It took me ages to prepare."

She tried to smile as he stuffed a couple of squares of kitchen roll into her hand. The tears dripped down. "I'm sorry."

"No, no. Keep talking. You don't think your mother likes you."

"No. Not very much."

Geraldine blew her nose, then crumpled the sheets of paper towel into a ball. He handed her more. "Go on. Blow again."

She blew again. "It's just the feeling I got," she told him. "Tonight, when I was sitting across from her, there was a moment when I felt like a child. As if the years had peeled away, and I was back to being young again, and she was back to being my mother."

"She *is* your mother, Geraldine."

"You know what I mean. Back to when no one has any choice but to think all the adults in their life somehow know better. And what was so horrid about this evening was that she definitely made it clear that she preferred Lulu."

"As she always has."

"No!" Geraldine said sharply. She took a moment or two to pull herself together. "At least, that's not what I believed. I mean, I know it looked that way to other people. To you. To your parents. Even to some of the people back at school. I'm not going to try to deny that she seemed to put Lulu first an awful lot of the time. But I did always think there must be reasons for it. That Lulu was a lot more vulnerable. Or Lulu was a sort of guest. Lulu had no one else."

"Neither did you."

"You know exactly what I mean. That was my *home*. I knew it. Everyone knew it. But Lulu was there by chance, and sort of under sufferance." She dumped another little ball of sodden paper on the table top. "But sitting on that sofa watching my mother tonight, I realized that she actually dislikes my personality. She thinks I'm dull. She thinks I'm smug. I realized that I'm not the sort of person my mother wants to be around. In actual fact, she truly *does* prefer Lulu, and I think she prefers her because she's more interesting and edgy. Unpredictable."

"Selfish and uncontrolled, I'd call it."

"Call it what you want. It's still what Mum prefers. I realized, driving back, that that is probably why she was attracted to my father. Because he was that way as well. Whipping us off from one weird place to another in that daft camper. Never giving a thought to where the next penny would come from. Even refusing to come back and live somewhere sensible when it was time for me to go to school. If Mum didn't have a soft spot for that sort of fecklessness, how come she stayed with Esteban as long as she did?" Pulling her plate back towards her, she added more cheerfully, "It would also explain why, after my dad pushed off back to Spain, she took up with someone like Jed. It all makes sense."

The storm cones clearly safely down again, he swept the tear-soaked balls of paper off the table and raised his glass. "Well, here's to the *orderly* life."

She offered him the smile he loved. "Yes, yes. The orderly life."

"Speaking of which, what sort of fit did your mother have when you let out the news that Linda is pregnant as well?"

"I never got that far."

"Really?" He peered at her curiously. "I don't know why not. After all, it does rather sound as if the two of you were talking for quite a time about Lulu and Harvey."

"We were. Pretty much all the time, in fact."

"And you told her your doubts. So how on earth did that little fact escape the conversation? I would have thought it might have been quite good for your mother to be reminded that people can be a little *too* —" he grinned, "'*mercurial*'."

He watched his wife search for an answer. And even then, as though still somewhat baffled herself, all she could say was, "Somehow it never seemed to be quite the right time. She was already sure that I was criticizing. Putting a blight on things. I tried to set her straight — told her that I'd be smiling at the wedding, popping champagne corks, and all that. But still I got the feeling she thought that I was being quite unnecessarily negative. I suppose, at heart, it was the same old story. I didn't want her thinking I was simply jealous. So, since the moment never came, I didn't push it."

While Geraldine rooted for yoghurt in the fridge, Robert cleared the plates. Clearly her natural buoyancy was back in force because, even before she returned to the table, she was adding, "And maybe it's for the best that I didn't mention it. I mean, when Harvey let the news slip, that might have been right at the start. So if this Linda has been very unlucky —" He heard the tiny intake of breath before she could press on, "or even changed her mind about going ahead — then anything I said about her ever having been pregnant at all would simply sound like hateful gossip."

"And might get back to Lulu."

"Who either doesn't want us to know or doesn't know herself." She gave a little shudder. "Oh God, I worry about that!"

He made the usual effort not to sound too dismissive of his stepsister-in-law's supposed vulnerability. "There's no need, Geraldine. We've been through this. You know as well as I do that even if Harvey had been exposed as a serial murderer when she was only three days overdue, Lulu would have carried on. She *wants* this baby." He couldn't help it. The contempt crept in. "And she's no reason to worry about the future. Everything always works out fine for our precious Lulu."

He worried that he might have sounded too unsympathetic. But then, passing behind her to put the serving plate back on the counter, he caught the harshness in her own muttered comment. "Doesn't it just!"

CHAPTER
NINE

Though Geraldine left several messages, it was at least another two weeks before Lulu was properly back in touch. Suddenly, without warning, she appeared on their doorstep. "Perhaps I should have rung. I know you're busy at weekends. But I was coming past, and wanted to ask your advice."

"Lovely to have you," Geraldine insisted. "And you look *radiant*. Clearly the pudding club suits you."

"I think it does," said Lulu. "I feel brilliant. I was a little tired at the start, but now I'm full of beans."

"So what's your problem?"

But Lulu somehow put off mentioning whatever it was that she had come to discuss. After a while, Geraldine dug out the iron and started on her blouses for the coming week. Just as she was getting desperate — would Lulu *never* stop talking about baby clothes and cots and nappies, and just get on with raising the subject that was bothering her? That, or get up and *go*? — Lulu lifted her pretty painted fingertips to her forehead and said, with all the falsity a brilliant actress like herself could muster, "Oh, God. I am sorry. I rather think I might be going to faint."

Geraldine felt she had no choice but to put down the iron and go through the motions. "Lulu? Are you all right?"

Her stepsister might have been playing Our Lady of the Camellias. "No, really! Don't worry. I just get a little dizzy sometimes."

"What can I get you? Water? A cup of tea?"

"Well, actually —" Lulu peeped through her fingers. "If you don't mind — if you could run to one tiny little sandwich . . ."

"Of course!"

So that was it, of course. She had to be invited to stay for lunch. It wasn't too much of a trial because, although Lulu kicked off with detailed accounts of how a couple of women in her antenatal class were dealing with their condition, Robert somehow managed to steer her off that topic on to her growing conviction that the gift shop in which she worked had now been doing so badly for so long that it was probably about to close. As she cleared away the plates, Geraldine took the chance to steal a sideways glance. So far as she could tell, Lulu had not yet begun to thicken out. But Linda, who'd been pregnant with the twins before, would surely change shape faster. Had Lulu just found out she wasn't carrying the only child Harvey would have for Christmas? Was this perhaps what she'd come round to talk about?

It was, of course, Robert who dared skate closest to the subject on both their minds. Suddenly breaking in on Lulu's litany of complaints about her employer, he asked her, "Anyway, how are things going? Is Linda managing? Is Harvey getting to see his children regularly? And how are you two finding sharing the flat?"

It seemed a wide enough set of questions to leave Lulu free to go down only avenues she chose. And, interestingly enough, she chose the last. "I didn't mind Harvey moving in," she told them. "That was fine by me. What I can't stand is that he has so many strong opinions about the bathroom."

"He wants to do it up?"

"No, no. The way we *use* it."

"Not following." He turned to Geraldine. "Are you?"

Geraldine shrugged. Inside her head, she was already drafting the next recruitment advert. After all, she couldn't be missing much by letting her attention slide. She couldn't recall a time when Lulu had chatted on so long about such inconsequential matters. Even now, rising from the table as though to help clear the plates, a single dish in hand, she had gone back to boring them about her bathroom. "You see, it's a bit of a mess. I simply dump my stuff where it's most handy. It is my place, after all. But Harvey has developed this fixation that all my 'war paint and woad', as he keeps calling it, should stay on one side of the basin, and he'll keep his things on the other." She barely hid the fact that, even as she spread her hands in such affected amazement, she was busy admiring her painted fingertips. "But I've got dozens of tubes and bottles and stuff. And he has practically nothing except his shaving gear, and he keeps most of that inside a bag. And . . ."

What was she *playing* at? If she was so determined to say nothing of any consequence, why on earth had she come? Just to prowl round the kitchen, inspecting the framed photographs on the wall, the clock and calendar, the notes pinned to the old cork board? On and on Lulu droned until, behind her back, Robert had taken to making strangulation signs. He couldn't turn away to load the dishwasher fast enough, while Geraldine took the chance to slink up to the bathroom for a short break. When she came down again, Lulu was still going on about the way that Harvey hated it when those small slivers of the last of the soap stuck to his flannel.

After she'd gone, Geraldine turned to Robert. "What was all *that* about?"

"You tell me. All I can say is, living with Harvey is doing her no good. Do you know, while I was scrubbing out that pan, she was actually telling me exactly how hot that benighted man likes to have the water while he is washing his face." He frowned. "Oh, yes. That cunning little brain of hers was definitely running on empty today. She seemed fine through the meal, while she was needling you about her pregnancy, and on about her job. But then, as soon as we got up from the table, she seemed to go into this tail spin of distraction." Like a detective, he gazed around the kitchen. "What *was* it? Any of the invitations?" He studied all the things they'd pinned to the cork board. The postcard from the vet reminding them that Puffer's shots were overdue. The dental appointment he still had to change. Holiday dates for the recycling collections.

Nothing there.

His eyes slid sideways to the all-year planner on which they marked everything else. Geraldine's trips down south to linked laboratory sites. Dana's engagement bash at Spoons. The dates for the annual graduate interviews. The summer party they threw every year for everyone who worked in their laboratory.

"She's up to something," he declared. "I know her backwards and I know she's up to something. But what can it be?"

The following week, Geraldine went round to her mother's to drop off the juicer Robert had borrowed. "He doesn't want to keep it. He says he's just like you — used it for four days, cut his finger washing it, and hasn't touched it since. He says you'll have to pass it on to someone else."

Jane Carter eyed the huge and gleaming gadget with both suspicion and distaste. "Oh, I don't know. I might try it again."

"You might," said Geraldine, and they both laughed.

Later, over their second coffee, Geraldine said, "How are things going with Lulu? Are you seeing much of her?"

"Not really," said her mother. "After all, she's still at work. She told me that she wants to carry on as long as she can."

With a lacing of mischief, Geraldine responded, "That won't be difficult. She only does three days a week."

"Two, now. She told me last week that, what with the way sales in the shop have been slipping, the owners have felt obliged to go back to doing the job themselves on Wednesdays."

"How on earth are they going to *manage?*"

Jane Carter looked mystified. "But, dear, why on earth shouldn't they? I'm sure they coped perfectly well before Lulu took over."

Geraldine stared. How could her mother have detached herself so much from the real problem that she could misunderstand a question like that? "Not the shop owners! Lulu and Harvey." Sensing her mother's sheer unwillingness to have the conversation ruffled in this way, she tried to defend her outburst. "I mean, for Harvey's wife to come to terms so amiably and quickly, she must have got a really good deal for herself and all the children."

"Not *all* the children," Mrs Carter said reprovingly. "Come now. He only has two."

"Only!" said Geraldine, hoping the sarcasm would gloss over her slip of the tongue. She stared out through the rain-streaked glass, wondering yet again why she'd not taken the chance to whisper to her mother the news that she and Robert had known for weeks. What stopped her? Could she really be protecting Harvey from his own idiotic indiscretion? Or Lulu, from hard truth? Or was the reason far more personal? Had all that business with the clinic left her so sensitive about other people's pregnancies that she could no longer blurt out the news of someone else's — even a stranger's — without some pain to herself?

"Geraldine?"

She forced her attention back. "What?"

"You're crying, darling."

"No, I'm not."

"I think you are, dear."

"Oh, God!" Geraldine scrubbed at the tears with the flat of her hand. "So I am. Sorry!"

Her mother leaned across to pat her knee as, one by one, more tears rolled down and dropped off Geraldine's chin on to the oh, so familiar hand, now deeply rivered with veins. "What is the *matter*, darling? Is something wrong? Is Lulu right about what she keeps saying?"

"No," Geraldine snapped automatically, before even asking, "Why, what *is* she saying?"

Mrs Carter lowered her head to check on Geraldine's expression as she came out with it. "She thinks that, though you won't admit it, even to yourself, deep down inside you're really, really upset because she's going to have a baby, and you're not." Jane Carter waited just a moment before persisting. "So is she right, dear? Is that it? Because, if it is, then I won't say a word, I promise you. You can tell me."

Oh, the temptation! Just to lean forward, let herself fall in those arms and howl, as she had howled her way back to comfort so many times through childhood. But how long would it be before a word let drop, even a special look of sympathy crossing her mother's face, assured her stepsister that she'd been right? A single day? A week?

Geraldine blew her nose, hard. "No, no. It's nothing like that." Quick! Find a lie! "It's just that . . ."

"Yes?"

"Oh, Mum. I know it sounds daft. I mean, I can't pretend that Lulu and I don't have our problems. She can get on my nerves so much when she's so selfish." Might as well sneak in one more hard truth while she had the chance. "*And* when she lashes out at people, even when they're doing her favours. But after all, it was a horrid life, wasn't it? Her mum getting ill in that appalling way, then being swept back to Peru with her by the relations." Getting into her stride, Geraldine blew her nose again and dared to lift her face. "And then Jed being mean enough to fight them to get Lulu back."

"I'm sure that Jed sincerely thought —"

But Geraldine didn't stop. "Then all that business of her being unsettled yet again when Jed brought her to live with us. That can't have been at all easy. *Or* having to leave again so suddenly, after Jed started drinking."

"*She* didn't have to leave. I made that perfectly clear to Jed when we split up. I was quite happy to carry on giving a home to Lulu."

"I didn't know that." (Don't get sidetracked now.) "But she *did* leave with him, didn't she? New place. New school, and all that. And then him dying in that horrible, *horrible* way, and nobody wanting her."

"Oh, Geraldine! *We* wanted her."

"Not really. *I* certainly didn't, and you knew that because I remember telling you."

Her mother's face went blank, and she said nothing. Clearly unwilling to confirm this version of events, she simply sat scraping away with a fingernail at some nonexistent flaw in the glaze of her coffee cup. Sufficiently irritated by her mother's determined self-deception to feel a bit more justified in covering her own tracks with self-serving cant, Geraldine pressed on. "So it's so *lovely* to see Lulu with this chance to find contentment at last. Getting a whole new start with Harvey and the baby. I know it must seem ridiculous — almost hypocritical, even, after all the things I've said about her over the years — but, if you really want to know, I think I'm crying because I'm so *happy* for her."

Oh, God! What a dreadful lie! About the worst she could have told. But she would *not* confess that the tears had come because she sometimes seemed to be the only person in the world who'd made an effort to create a settled life with a responsible and loving husband, then couldn't have her own child. It wasn't *fair*. Or right. The world should run along more sensible lines. And how could she explain this to her mother, who was so weak and soft? The very first time Lulu sent out one of her cunning feelers, Jane Carter would be bound to tack and weave, and finally come out with some incriminating give-away. "Well, now you mention it, I do believe that, deep inside, she can't help being just a little jealous. Poor dear. Why, when we were having coffee only last week . . ."

It was the last thing Geraldine could bear. False sympathy from Lulu. That would drive her *mad*.

"Oh, God!" she said again. "Oh, please don't tell her I am being so wet that I'm weeping for happiness for her. I mean, she probably isn't in the mood for that sort of rapture anyway, what with feeling so nauseous. And aren't the poor things still having to hang about, waiting for the divorce?"

It was as if her mother, too, was pleased the conversation had been steered on to firmer ground. "I think they are. But Lulu told me that she thinks he'll soon be getting a date for the decree nisi."

"Nisi? That's just the first bit, isn't it?"

Another disingenuous contribution, since she and Robert had checked these matters on the internet and even worked through all the possible timings of Harvey's divorce over the previous weeks. But it was a simple question, and she had earned a breather.

Her mother nodded. "Yes. And after that he has to wait another six weeks till it's all finalized."

Did she remember from divorcing Jed? But that had been years ago, and it was unlikely that that bombastic and aggressive drunk had ever helped to make wheels turn — except, of course, the ones that spun beneath him on the evening that he drove into that stone parapet.

A nasty thought. Somewhat ashamed of herself, Geraldine turned back to the subject in hand. "Does Lulu talk to you a lot about the way it's going?"

"No, no. From time to time she has let something drop, of course. Like last week, when some letter with a court date had just arrived, and she was grumbling to me that it would ruin some arrangement to go out shopping. Then Harvey told her it was merely a formality. He didn't have to be there."

"Harvey would know."

Mrs Carter ignored the jibe. "And I don't care to press for any details."

"In case it sounds nosy?"

"In case she thinks that we're all queuing up to come to a wedding." She waved a hand at Geraldine. "I mean, look at you! Already weeping with happiness because Lulu is finally settling down. Don't think I don't know how many sacrifices you've had to make to try to get along with her — especially when you were young. I'm sure we can all remember how difficult she sometimes made things."

Always, thought Geraldine, still smiling at her mother. Be honest. Get it right, Mum. How difficult she *always* made things.

"And, darling, you've been wonderful all along. So patient. And so generous-spirited." Jane Carter reached across to squeeze her daughter's hand. "Oh, you can't fool me, dear. I know you very well indeed. And I know *exactly* how happy and fulfilled you're going to feel the day you watch her finally marry Harvey."

CHAPTER
TEN

"I felt *disgusted* with myself," Geraldine told Robert a few hours later. "Totally disgusted. I mean, there she was, going on about how *sweet* I was . . ."

She shuddered.

"I sometimes wonder about your mother," Robert said. "Has she no memory at all? Does she truly not recall how Lulu used to drip bleach on your clothes, and hide your knickers on examination mornings? How she'd 'forget' to pass on messages from all your friends, but never miss the chance of telling you every snide bit of gossip she ever heard about you — not to mention plenty she didn't. God, even a couple of years ago she was putting on that bloody 'look-at-me-fainting' act of hers just as your mother and I were trying to watch you get that medal."

"Oh, please. We will be up all night if you embark on Lulu's roll of dishonour."

"Exactly! So how can your mother possibly believe that standing there watching the person who made you so miserable for so long stroll up the aisle with the new love of her life will be the sacred and happy culmination of all your wishes?" He shook his head in simple disbelief. "How could she *possibly* be daft enough to believe *that's* why you were crying?"

Geraldine thought that she might know the answer, but Robert was still ploughing on. "No. I think it's much more likely that you were so distracted and upset that you misunderstood." He grinned. "In fact, I reckon maybe she was being a bit sarcastic."

"*Sarcastic?*"

"Why not? I know your mother always takes very good care to keep her own counsel —"

"To make sure she keeps her life unruffled," Geraldine corrected sourly.

"Perhaps. But maybe she really *does* know exactly how happy and fulfilled you'll feel the day you watch your stepsister put her official stamp upon the ruination of three young children's lives."

"We don't *know* there are three," Geraldine fretted. "Linda might have changed her mind about her pregnancy."

"Two, three . . . It's still a future stuffed with problems, isn't it? We know that from your own experience. Either the poor mites will have one harried, overtired parent, or they will get the usual grim procession of steps and halves, and wicked this and thats."

"My mother wasn't wicked. If anything, she was a sight *too* kind."

He took her hand. "You really are beginning to think that, aren't you?"

"I've *always* thought that."

"Yes. But the same old thought has suddenly begun to make you angry."

Geraldine considered. "You're right," she said. "That's what's gone wrong. My feelings about Lulu are spreading out. Up until now, I've almost managed to keep my mother out of it. I've told myself she didn't have much choice, what with Jed dying like that, and Lulu having no one else to take her in. But she did, really."

"Yes, she did."

"Your parents knew that, didn't they? Your mother always said that, in my mother's shoes, she would have sent Lulu back to her family in Peru. Or into foster care."

"My mother still says that."

For just a moment the two of them sat quietly, imagining Eileen and Trevor Forsley sitting contentedly on their balcony in Melbourne, still disapproving of Lulu.

"Your mother hated Lulu, didn't she?"

He shrugged. "Not hated, no. But she did think that Lulu was given far too many chances, and you were the loser in that family. We all thought that."

"Yes, well, I think that too, now," Geraldine explained. "I think that's why I started to cry. Because I suddenly realized that Mum was never going to allow herself to have a clue about the damage that her weakness did to me. If she'd stood up to Lulu, my whole life would have been different."

"Not your whole life," he hastened to remind her. "Not your whole life."

"Well, no. I'm happy now, of course."

He laughed. "You look it!"

"You know what I mean. But I am suddenly as angry at my mother as I am at Lu. More, in fact. Because Lulu can't help being who she is, but Mum could have stopped her from being it under our roof." The first tear rolled. It was as if she didn't even notice it. Had she wept all the way home? "But Mum was so busy bending over backwards for Lulu that I came a very poor second. Because I have a little self-control, she took advantage. And it wasn't *fair*."

"No. And we all knew that next door." He gave her a comforting squeeze. "But that's all over now."

He was astonished when she brushed him off. "It isn't, though! That's the whole point! Because I can't help *wanting* something from my mother now. Not an apology. Not even a confession. I just would like my mother to make the effort to acknowledge, in some small, tiny way, that she does know how ghastly Lulu was, and how it was so awful for me." She looked quite fierce. "I don't want her to keep on *lying* to herself." She stepped back suddenly, rather like someone on a stage giving herself a little more room before launching into some grand soliloquy. He watched in consternation as she affected that soft baffled look he'd seen so often on his mother-in-law's face, and made her voice sound helpless. What was she doing? Apeing one of her mother's regular whitewashings of their mutual past? Yes. There was the heavy sigh. " 'Oh, yes. Lulu could be quite *difficult* at times. It wasn't always easy!' " Her imitation done, Geraldine's expression snapped back to one so angry he didn't recognize it as her own. She practically spat. "How *dare* she? How dare she blank out everything she doesn't choose to know? How dare she just rewrite her own daughter's life simply to suit herself?" He waited through the strange short silence. Clearly his wife had something more to say. "I tell you, I could forgive her if just once — just once — she could stand up on *my* side. Stand up for *me*. For *me*."

He took her in his arms to try to stop her trembling. But it was hopeless. She could not be comforted. And in the end he just gave up, and let her cry and cry.

"Why don't you talk to her about it?" he asked a few days later, when it was evident that she was feeling stronger, and back on top.

"I might," said Geraldine. But in the end, she talked to Lulu first. Lulu had rung that morning, just as the two of them were making for the door. "Can I come round? I need to borrow Puffer."

"Puffer? What for?"

"Photo shoot. Something to do with sofas. These people of Harvey's need a fat lazy cat."

"Well, Puffer's your man. But I'm afraid he's out right now. And we're just off to work."

"Bugger. Hold on a tick."

Impatiently Geraldine waited through Lulu's muffled discussion with Harvey about the deadline. Then, suddenly she was back. "Right, then. I'll fetch him early this evening."

"Actually that's not —"

But Lulu had hung up.

By the time Lulu came round to fetch him, shortly after six, Puffer was not only back again but fast asleep.

"Auditioning," Robert explained. "He isn't getting up to greet you because he would prefer to stay in character."

"I knew he was the perfect cat." Lulu was cock-a-hoop. "These people who want him are trying to get the filming of their advert done on the cheap."

"No point in renting a professional for this job," Robert said. "No one lies in a coma on a sofa quite like our Puffer."

"Dead right," said Lulu, plonking herself down beside him in such a flamboyantly exhausted manner that Geraldine felt obliged to offer tea.

"Herbal, please," Lulu said, making it sound like an order in a restaurant.

Still irritated from the brusque ending to the morning's phone call, Geraldine spent the time in the kitchen bracing herself to make her stepsister earn the mug of steaming camomile she handed over. "Lu, there's something I've been meaning to ask you for ages."

"Oh, yes. What's that?"

"It's an odd question . . ."

Lulu's head reared back, rather alarming Geraldine until she realized that her stepsister was simply recoiling from the heat of the tea. "Well, go on. Fire ahead."

"I suddenly started to wonder . . . What did you actually *think* of the times when you were living with us?"

Lulu screwed up her pretty face. "What do you mean?"

Geraldine pressed on. "Well, I was curious about your feelings. I was just wondering how you felt about suddenly having a sister, and then not having her again, and then having her back."

"Do you mean you?"

"Who else?" said Geraldine, and laughed. "Unless, of course, your dad led yet another double life from the one Mum found out about."

Lulu was laughing too, now. "Oh, that was terrible. Do you remember all that awful clunking and banging?"

"God, yes!"

Robert lifted his head from the laboratory reports that he'd been working on while he was eavesdropping. "Do I know about this?"

They both ignored him. Suddenly it seemed as if all the years between had slid away, and they were once again sisters together. "There we were, silent as mice in those twee little twin beds!"

"Horrid pink downie covers! Ugh!"

"Both of us absolutely convinced that he was killing her."

Now Lulu was pointing. "You thought that he was chopping up her body!"

"No madder than you! You thought that he was nailing it into a box."

"What are you *on* about?" Robert persisted, but neither of them bothered to break off to explain.

"If she'd just raised her voice! It wouldn't have taken much for us to realize she was still alive. How long did we lie there worrying?"

"I can't remember. I bet it was at least a couple of hours. I'm quite surprised we didn't go to look."

"How could we? We were *terrified*. You were, as well, you know. It wasn't only me."

"I was. I really was."

"I didn't know any of this," said Robert. "How come no one ever told me?"

Geraldine finally turned his way. "You knew that Jed went off after some giant row about that floozie-boots."

"Jasmine," remembered Lulu. Both of them laughed again.

"And you knew he came back next day to pick up Lulu."

"Yes," Robert said. "But I didn't know about this lying-in-bed-imagining-murder business."

"There's not much to it," Geraldine explained. "It's just that we lay in the dark, each of us thinking the other must be asleep. And in the end we heard the front door banging. Both of us sat up to look out the window, and there was Lulu's dad heaving his gear into the back of a taxi."

"You thought it was her body even then! Stuffed in his kit bag!"

He stared as the two of them chuckled together. Small wonder that his wife found it so hard to keep Lulu in check, if running through her life, like letters through a stick of rock, were memories like this.

"Then Mum came out to lend him twenty quid to pay the fare, so we knew she was still alive. Then we went back to sleep."

Feeling a sudden need to remind Geraldine of her stepsister's flaws, he asked Lulu, "What, straight away? Weren't you at all worried about him?"

She shrugged. "Not really, no. And anyway, he was back next day, after he'd found some place for me and him to live."

"I do remember him taking you away," admitted Robert. "As I recall, my parents kept a very beady eye on him over the fence in case things suddenly turned nasty, and they had to rush in to rescue Jane. Then, almost in a moment, you were gone, and none of us saw you for ages."

"Four years," said Geraldine.

"Was it that long?" Lulu shrugged. "Well, that's how it goes. Par for the course. You people who come from settled families have no idea."

"So answer Geraldine's question," Robert ordered her. "How did you *feel*?"

"About living in their house?" She made a little face. "It was all right. I mean, her mum was very kind. But I did feel that Geraldine always got the best of things."

Geraldine took care to check that Lulu's nose was deep in her mug again before she dared exchange a look with Robert. "Really? You think I got the best of things? *Always*?"

"Pretty much. And you did, you know. You can't deny it. All of those brilliant reports, and all those sodding prizes."

"Those were not things I *got*," said Geraldine. "They were things that I *worked* for. If you had ever put your mind to it, you could have had them too."

"Oh, I don't know," said Lulu.

She sounded so flippant that, once again, Geraldine felt a rush of irritation. How could her stepsister sit there so complacently, claiming she'd been the one to be short-changed?

Sensing the rising tension, Robert hastily stepped in. "Well, what about all those years earlier, when you first came? Way back in primary school, before Geraldine started to annoy you by winning all those prizes? How did you feel back then?"

"Just as resentful, I expect."

"And what was your reason that time?"

"I don't know." She turned to Geraldine. "You again, probably."

"Oh, me, of course."

Lulu was grinning. "Well, Geraldine, you must admit that you were horribly annoying. A ghastly Goody-Goody-Two-Shoes. Little Miss Perfect. I mean, I was a bit of a weasel, I admit, with all those lies, and trying to get you into trouble all the time. But at least I was *human*. You were just like a china doll."

"A china doll? Hardly!"

"Oh, I don't mean in *looks*," said Lulu scornfully. "I mean in your *expression*."

"Lulu —" warned Robert. But she'd already brushed him off. He'd lit the fuse after all, and clearly now there was to be no stopping her. "You know what china dolls look like. We had some rather good replicas in the shop a couple of months ago. They kept reminding me of you."

Giving up any attempt to put the brakes on Lulu, Robert turned his warning glance on Geraldine. Taking the hint, she only murmured, "Oh, really? Did they?"

"They certainly did. They drove me mad, in fact. We sold the lot, and I've been very careful to make sure none of the offers to restock have got through to Tara." She peeped at Geraldine over her mug of herbal tea. "It was their porcelain faces that drove me mad. Just like that bland expression you keep putting on. You're doing it now. Just like your mother, in fact. In this respect, the two of you are exactly the same. You could be absolute *twins*."

"Well," Robert said. "Time to shift Puffer, I suppose." Geraldine watched as he scooped the grey furry lump up in his arms and carried him, apparently still sleeping, into the kitchen, where she had put the cat carrier for Lulu to use. To her surprise, instead of hearing Puffer's usual furious yowling as he was shoved into the cramped wire cage, she heard the back door open.

And then close.

Well, good for Robert. No longer feeling any need to hit back at Lulu, Geraldine waited in silence until her husband came back in, picking cat hairs off his sweater.

Casually, Lulu unwound herself and rose from the sofa. "Oh, well, better be off. Is he all safely in that carrier thing?"

Robert stopped in his tracks. "Whoops!" he said. "Oh, I'm so sorry, Lulu! What you were saying was so

100

fascinating that I got carried away and clean forgot you wanted Puffer for that photo shoot. So I've just put him out, and now the chances are he won't be back till morning. What a shame!"

CHAPTER
ELEVEN

When the phone rang a couple of hours later, it never occurred to either of them that it could be Lulu again, so Geraldine picked up without even checking.

"Is that you, Geraldine? Oh, God! I've just had a phone call! Harvey's gone back to Linda!"

She sounded so distraught that Geraldine pointed Robert to the other phone. He hurried to fetch it, then they stood across from one another, listening.

"He'd only gone round there to see the kids. When I got back from you there was a message on the answerphone saying that he and Linda had been talking, and he would be a little late."

"What time did he leave that?"

"Somewhere round six, I think. And then he rang again a couple of hours later to tell me to go ahead and eat. And now he's just this minute rung and told me he's not coming back!"

"Tonight? Or not at all?"

It was a full-blooded wail. "Not at all! Not ever!"

"Oh, my Lord," Geraldine gasped. "Did he say why?"

"Oh, yes!" The wail was now half misery, half outrage. "He says that Linda has just told him that she is pregnant."

Across the room, Robert was raising an eyebrow at Geraldine. She gave him one short warning frown, and said to Lulu, "You realize I can hardly believe what I am hearing."

"Oh, yes!" said Lulu. Her voice was thick with scorn. "Apparently he feels he ought to stay with her to see it through."

"Perhaps the —" Geraldine nearly said "slimeball", before remembering how often in the last few years Harvey had slunk back to his wife, and then returned. Hastily she revised her response. "Perhaps the man's conveniently forgotten that you are pregnant too."

"The trouble is," wailed Lulu, "that she's more pregnant than I am! Can you believe that? Linda is five months gone!"

"Oh, this gets worse and worse," said Geraldine. And Robert didn't help. Abandoning his tactful silence, he said to Lulu, "Perhaps the bastard's back on one of his great etiquette trips. Do you remember how he couldn't leave his wife, except on Thursdays? I expect now he thinks the right thing to do is chum Linda through her labour, then come back afterwards to do the same for you."

Geraldine glared at him. "Oh, shut up, Robert. This isn't helping."

Lulu was howling now. "Oh, I can't bear it. I can't *bear* it! I am so *angry* with him. Can't we send Robert round there to bloody well root him out and bash him up?"

Bash him up? Geraldine had barely heard the expression since she left primary school. She glanced across at Robert as she warned Lulu, "I'm not sure the headline 'MAN BEATEN TO A PULP FOR GOING BACK TO PREGNANT WIFE AND KIDS' would play that well. Listen, why don't I come round there to pick you up and bring you back here for the night?" She took the fact that Lulu started snivelling as an agreement. "You wait there, Lu. Be careful not to answer any calls, and I'll be round in less than twenty minutes."

"Thirty," insisted Robert. "Unless you're planning on smashing yourself to pieces somewhere around the bypass."

He had forgotten about Jed's fatal crash. Poor Lulu howled again. "For God's sake!" Geraldine snapped at her husband. "Put down that phone and shut your bloody mouth."

It was the rudest she had ever been to him.

He was still staring after her, astonished and ashamed, as she swept up her car keys and ran out.

The phone call was a brief one, and neither Geraldine nor Robert heard a word of it because, while Lulu was downstairs on the sofa taking it, they were busy arguing with one another up on the landing. "You have to *tell* her," Robert was insisting. "You have to tell her that he's known for weeks. If you don't put her straight on what a louse he is, I will."

"For God's sake! How can I tell her now?" Geraldine hissed back. "Just as the first shock's over, and the cramps have stopped. And anyhow, he's probably going to put her straight himself."

104

"What makes you think that? His astonishing track record for utter honesty?"

"I just think that he might."

"I wash my hands of it," said Robert. "I am *exhausted*. Since you can't see sense, I'm going off for a bath."

"Perhaps as well, given you're not being helpful."

He stayed locked in the bathroom until pangs of hunger drove him downstairs in his dressing gown, towards the fridge. Just as he passed the back door, a steady pounding started up. Harvey was on the step.

"Fuck off," said Robert, opening up.

For once in his lifetime, Harvey made an attempt to come in promptly.

"I said, 'Fuck off,'" said Robert. "So fuck off."

Harvey demanded, equally irritably, "Why did you open the door, then?"

"To let in my cat." Robert leaned out into darkness. "Puffer! Puffer, where are you? Come in at once. It's bedtime."

"Be quiet, both of you," said Geraldine, coming into the kitchen. "You'll wake the whole damn street." She turned to Harvey. "You can come in," she said. "But only because Lulu wants me to let you. Robert and I are going off to bed. And you are not to wake us up with any more of your comings or goings or arguments."

"Or sex," warned Robert as Geraldine hauled him off towards the stairs. Even before they'd left the room, Harvey had started. They heard each word as they went up the stairs. "Oh, God! I'm so sorry, Lu! How can you ever forgive me? I'm such a fool. The thing is, Lulu, she was standing there, all fat and podgy round the middle, crying her eyes out and saying how she couldn't cope, and how Eddie was acting up all the time, being a perfect *monster*, and how small boys, especially, really need their father. And I just lost my head and —"

Geraldine shut the bedroom door.

"Hey!" Robert said. "Excuse me. I was listening to that."

"It's not your business," Geraldine assured him.

"Maybe it's not, but I am interested."

"Well, interest yourself in something else, because this door's staying shut."

"All right," he offered. "You come over here, and I will interest myself in you."

She paused, considering. And then she made her offer. "All right. But on one condition. That I don't hear either of the names Lulu or Harvey from your lips until tomorrow morning."

"Done!" Cheerfully he pulled her down beside him on the bed and started on her hooks and zips and buttons. "Excellent deal all round."

When Geraldine woke up, there was a note on the table. "Thanks. You were angels. Going home now. Lulu." She'd put a row of kisses underneath. Geraldine left the note where Robert would see it when the alarm woke him half an hour later, and drove off to Crewe to meet laboratory suppliers.

When she got home, there was no message from Lulu; and when Robert banged through the door about an hour after that, she was still wondering whether or not to phone her.

"Have you seen Puffer?" Robert asked.

Geraldine shook her head.

"He's got a cheek, that cat," said Robert. "After we've rescued him from all the horrors of the life of a celebrity. Aren't pets supposed to earn their keep by being home to welcome you back from a hard day at work?"

"That's dogs."

"Well, let's get one of those. They're much, much better than cats anyhow. Brainier. And far more beautiful."

She realized he was on this riff only because he'd spotted Puffer tucked away behind their fattest cushion. "He isn't *listening*," she pointed out.

"A common fault in this extended family," sighed Robert. "Has she been in touch?"

"I think I was standing here wondering whether it would have killed her to phone us."

"You mean, after ruining our evening and keeping us up half the night?"

"That sort of thing."

"Nonsense! So long as *Lulu*'s happy ..." He grinned. "But you could phone your mother to complain about her, and get the gossip that way."

"Why me?"

"Because, my dove, it will look far more natural."

"Oh, so we're still on that?"

"Aren't we?" He came across and stood in front of her. "Or have you had enough?" He studied her face.

"It's getting to you, isn't it? All of these pregnant ladies milling around us? You're finding it harder than you thought to keep acting casual."

"I am a bit. Especially when I see that you're reduced to trying to tease a cat into calling out, 'Welcome home, Daddy!'"

The blow hit home. He didn't smile. "God, what a pair we are. I know. We'll have a cup of tea, and then we'll emigrate."

She certainly wasn't in the mood to say, "But what about my mother?" But she did go to phone her. "Any word from Lulu?"

"No, dear. Why? Is there something wrong?"

Clearly she hadn't heard. But Lulu had slapped on no embargo about telling her. So here at last was Geraldine's chance to set the record straight. It was such worrying news she thought she'd try to break it gently. "Well, you see, last night there was a really big wobble. It seems —"

Clearly her mother didn't choose to be perturbed. She couldn't break in fast enough. "Oh, Geraldine. Let's face it. Pregnant women! They are all over the place emotionally. I expect that things are perfectly all right again now."

"It was to do with Harvey, actually."

"Oh, well. Things can't be at all easy for him, either, right at the moment."

When would her mother *ever* stop making excuses for people's bad behaviour? "Easy or not, Mum, he has behaved disgracefully."

"Geraldine —"

"And now his chickens have come home to roost, because —"

"Geraldine! Whatever you think of Harvey, he is about to become part of our family. So I hope that, whatever it is that you're going to say about him, you will at least try to be *kind*."

For just a moment, Geraldine was too angry to speak. But then she thought it through. Finish the call, she urged herself. Don't say another word. As soon as Lulu comes round howling her eyes out, she'll realize what it was that you were trying to tell her, and she'll feel *awful*. So just go ahead. *Punish* her.

"Whoops!" she said, not even trying to pretend she was sincere. "Is that the time? I really should have been somewhere by now."

She put the phone down gently and stood there looking at it for a while, tempted to pick it up again and bang it on the table. Then she stormed off into the kitchen, where she caught Robert holding the sweetest little woollen baby hat in cheery stripes. The thing was conical, and it had tiny earflaps.

Her husband spun round guiltily. "Sorry! I thought you would be longer on the phone."

"Ha!" Geraldine said sourly. She reached out for the tiny knitted hat, and her mood changed. "That's *sweet*. It's absolutely *darling*. Where on earth did you find it?"

"Charity shop. I think it's from Peru."

"It's quite enchanting."

"I wasn't going to show you," Robert admitted. "But I was walking past, and it was there, and I thought, what with poor Lulu having such a night of it . . ."

109

"Why not?" said Geraldine. "After all, whatever that louse does, she will still have to keep the baby now."

He did the maths himself. "Yes, I suppose she will." Relieved that his purchase didn't appear to be causing his wife distress, Robert reached over to the jar on the counter, pulled out their longest wooden spoon and stuck the baby hat on top of it.

"Sweet!" Geraldine said again. "I think Lulu will love it."

"I'll find some wrapping paper."

"No, no. Let me."

He was surprised. This wasn't the sort of task that Geraldine usually took off his hands. But off she went with the hat, and he turned his attention to thinking about supper. "Fancy a pizza?" he called after her, but she was out of hearing, and by the time he'd followed her upstairs, the phone was ringing.

He watched as Geraldine tossed the little hat aside and sat on the bed. "Yes, of *course* we were wondering, Lulu. So how did it go?"

Pizza, then. And his choice. Whistling, he went off to slide one of the deep-pan pepperonis she would never choose into the oven, and make a salad. It must have been a lengthy enough call because by the time that she was back, supper was ready.

"So? What's the story?"

"Typical Harvey. It seems that he went over as usual to see the kids, with nothing awful in mind. But Linda was in a stew and dead pissed off because her washing machine was leaking all over the floor, and little whatsisname — you know, the fierce one —"

"Eddie."

"Yes, Eddie. Well, he was having tantrums, and sneakily lashing out at his brother with his feet, and stuff like that."

"A typical family homecoming, presumably." He grinned. "Perhaps I do prefer to come back to Puffer."

"Anyhow, that's when he phoned the first time, to say he'd be a little late." She reached for the salad spoons he was offering. "But Lulu says that only a few minutes after he'd put down the phone to deal with Eddie, Linda burst into tears and told him that she was pregnant."

They sat in silence until Robert said, "He is an *arsehole*, isn't he? He's such a bloody liar. How long ago was it that he told me?"

"Weeks."

"*Weeks*."

Geraldine shivered. "And I suppose that he's been spending most of them nagging poor Linda to get rid of it."

"Come off it, Geraldine. The man's so spineless he will simply have been hanging around, hoping that's what she'd decide."

"Or that she'd lose it naturally."

He shuddered. "Creep! But now she's so far gone, I suppose even Harvey can't keep on pretending to himself that it's not going to happen. My Christ, what a mess! Is Lulu still devastated?"

"Well, that's the strange thing. I can't work it out. I mean, when she came round here she was as shocked and horrified as you'd expect."

"God, yes. I've never seen her in that state before."

"But now she's different. I wondered if she had decided she was going to stay with him, and was just keeping her end up." She caught Robert's baffled look. "You know — by seeming not to find the whole business nearly as appalling —"

He stepped into her hesitation. "As she clearly did last night? And we made it clear that we did too?"

"That's right. Lulu is taking a very different line now. As if it isn't a big deal at all. Almost to be expected."

"Even the pregnancy? Oh, well." He shrugged. "I suppose she couldn't have assumed he *never* slept with Linda before he left."

"Whatever she thought, he has already worked her round to making light of it. Honestly, she was telling the story almost as if it was funny. And totally from Harvey's point of view." Wrinkling her nose, she peeled off all her pepperoni circles, and put them on the rim of her plate. "She told me how, after we vanished up to bed, he threw himself on her mercy, trying to explain how while he was standing there in that great puddle on the floor, with all the mess and noise and chaos, he suddenly felt so sorry for poor Linda he couldn't bear it."

"And that's presumably when he rang the second time. To tell Lulu to go on and eat?"

"That's right. He said he felt he couldn't simply stroll away and leave Linda to cope while things were in such a state. He thought it was his duty to spend the evening there."

112

Lifting Geraldine's pepperoni circles from her plate, Robert piled them on to what was left of his own pizza. "And Lulu didn't go wild?"

"Well, she says not. In fact, she seemed to be trying for the moral high ground. She claimed she thought that it reflected rather well on Harvey that he should make such efforts to pitch in and help."

"Even though he and Linda are now within three weeks of their divorce?"

He'd startled her. "And how do you know that?"

"Because I'm counting. I am keeping track. Go on. So there he is, trying to get his wife's hall floor scrubbed nice and clean before the envelope with the decree absolute falls through the letterbox on to it."

His scathing tone surprised her. "You would do that for me. You'd be as kind as Harvey was to Linda if we were having a divorce."

"Don't!" he warned. "Don't even say the word. And don't you ever again put my good name in any sentence that has that bastard's in it." As quickly as it had turned harsh, his tone switched back. "So," he said. "Onwards and upwards with this astonishing story. There he is, back with Linda . . ."

She thought it better to ignore his outburst. "Pulling the stops out, it seems. Lulu's so daft, she almost sounded proud of his achievements. She says he sorted out the kids and fixed the washing machine."

"*Harvey?*"

"It seems all it needed was to be pulled away from the wall. Once it was out, it was quite obvious that one of the feeder hoses had slipped off."

113

"One that he fitted in the first place, I have no doubt."

"Yes, I expect so. Anyhow, that's when he phoned Lulu the third time with all that stuff that she was telling us last night."

"Oh, yes. That he can't do it to Linda. That he would feel a rat. Telling poor Lulu that he's not coming back at all, then slamming down the phone before she's even had a chance to *speak*."

"That's about it, though even that has had a little airbrushing since we first heard it. And after that, it seems, he and Linda worked as the fine team they can be to put the kids to bed, and then sit down to have a well-earned bite of supper."

"Supper? Oh, yes! I bet!"

"Yes, I thought that. But anyway, that's what he's telling Lulu."

"Well, I suppose they are still married — just. And he can't get her pregnant over again, not at the moment. So it was probably safe."

She didn't smile. She just went on with Lulu's story. "But then it seems that Eddie — or maybe it was the other one —"

"Barney."

"Yes, it was Barney. He woke with a nightmare. Screaming and thrashing — it was the works and he was inconsolable. Even Harvey admits that it took ages to calm him. Then Barney wanted a hot-chocolate drink, so Linda sent Harvey down to make it." Geraldine grinned for the first time since she'd begun the whole sorry tale. "And that's where Act Two begins, because Harvey claims that he was only downstairs for a little while — a couple of minutes at most. But Linda's take on it, apparently, was that the man was gone so long — for nearly twenty minutes — that she suspected him of being back on the phone."

"To Lulu?"

"I suppose. Anyhow, instead of yelling down at him from upstairs and waking Eddie, the woman ended up having to dig poor Barney out of bed to carry him downstairs. And then —" She grinned again. "Guess!"

"I can't," he said despairingly. "I simply can't."

"Harvey was sitting calmly at the kitchen table, reading the paper!"

Robert was staring.

"And that, it seems," Geraldine finished up, "was when Linda finally came to her senses, and threw the weaselly little bastard out again."

"Blimey! The man just seems to *beg* for it, doesn't he?" Shunting the debris of pizza crusts into a pile, he added, "So what time was that?"

"About an hour after I brought Lulu round to us."

"You're telling me that, after upsetting her like that, the stupid wanker sat in her flat till nearly midnight, waiting for her to come home, and didn't even guess where she would be?"

"So it seems."

He shook his head in wonder, and then said cheerfully, "What a great marriage this is going to be."

CHAPTER
TWELVE

Jane Carter rang early next morning in a real panic. "Geraldine, Lulu tells me that you and Robert already know this awful news about Linda."

Geraldine kept her voice even. "Yes, we do. It's what I kept trying to tell you."

Her mother brushed the rebuke aside. "What are we going to *do*?"

"Do?"

"Well, surely . . ." But even she was flummoxed. "Oh, I don't know! I'm so confused I don't know where I am."

"Well, I know where *I* am," said Geraldine. "I'm standing here, stark naked, in front of my closet. And I am going to have to go to work. Can I please phone you later?"

"Oh, if you would, dear!"

Geraldine softened. "I do agree, it is all a bit of a mess."

"A *bit* of a mess?" But clearly it struck even Jane that the one person who could not be charged with playing Lulu's problems down was her stepsister. "I'm beginning to think that you've been right all along, and

Harvey comes wrapped in a disquieting amount of trouble."

"Oh, I don't know," said Geraldine. "You must remember that we should be *kind*."

Instantly Robert's hand reached round to prise the phone out of her hand. "Jane?" he said easily. "You won't mind me breaking in, will you? But Geraldine can't talk now. She isn't even dressed, and has to get me to the station in time for a train. I swear that she'll get back to you as soon as she can." He put the phone down. "Geraldine, that was *naughty*."

"Oh, come on. I was only teasing her."

"And she deserves it. But you know that from now on she and the poor wronged mother-to-be will be even more in cahoots. If you let out a shadow of spite, it will get back to Lulu."

"I suppose so."

"And we don't want that." He put his hand under her chin and turned her face to him. "Do we?"

She had a think about it. "No. We don't."

"Right, then. So you just carry on looking innocent, and keep your trap shut. And, whatever you do, don't crow 'I told you so' to either Jane or Lulu. There's no need in any case. They both already *know*."

That cheered her up. "That's true. Even my mother can't pretend she has forgotten that I've been warning everyone right from the start."

It made it easier, halfway through the morning, to make the call. Brushing the last of the crumbs from Martin's ginger biscuits off the front of her blouse, she reached for the phone on the lab bench. Her mother answered on the second ring. "So," Geraldine began without preamble, "straight to the topic of the day?"

"Oh, this is awful."

"Yes. Awful."

"My heart goes out to her."

"How was she when you spoke to her?" Geraldine asked curiously.

"Very subdued."

Ah, so her stepsister's gung-ho reaction to the news was wearing off. "Yes, it'll be a while before she gets over this one."

"Yes, I agree. I think the poor girl's going to feel *very* outshone."

Had she heard that one right? " 'Outshone'?"

"You know. What with the other baby being born less than a month before hers."

Geraldine's sheer astonishment robbed her of any sensible response. In any case, her mother was already pressing on. "And Lulu's very worried about something else."

Thank God for that, thought Geraldine. "Oh, yes. And what is that?"

"She's worried that Linda might have a little girl, and she'll just have a boy."

" '*Just*'?"

Her mother did at least have the grace to sound embarrassed. "Well, clearly, 'the more angels, the more room for them', and all of that. Still . . ."

"Still — what?"

"Well, dear," said Mrs Carter somewhat reprovingly, as if she thought her daughter was being quite

118

unnecessarily insensitive, "Harvey does have two little sons already."

"Oh, so he has," said Geraldine. "How very silly of me. I hadn't thought he might not want to be bothered with a third."

"Geraldine —"

"Not if he has a little daughter in the other house to dandle on his knee."

"Geraldine, I'm not sure that —"

Oh, she was so, so near the edge. Best to draw back. "Sorry," she interrupted hastily, for all the world as if she meant it. "I'm obviously completely at sea. I thought from what you said that that was Lulu's major worry. And I was *sympathizing*."

"It sounded more to me as if you might have been being a little sarcastic."

"No, not at all." She forced herself to muddy her tracks. "Well, perhaps a little. Only at Harvey, though."

Jane Carter sighed. "You really do have a bit of a down on Harvey, don't you, Geraldine? I know he can be tiresome with all that nattering about blocked roads and little back routes he's so sure no one else knows about. But you have got to admit that his heart's in the right place, and he has settled Lulu down, and made her happy."

"Oh, yes," said Geraldine, remembering her stepsister hunched on the sofa, staring down at the carpet through smudged and hollow eyes. "He makes her very happy."

It was an olive branch. And Mrs Carter's natural optimism about her stepdaughter's affairs came flooding back. "And we can't really say that all this news about Linda is *such* a dreadful thing. He could, after all, have been the father of three children from the very start."

"Girls *or* boys," Geraldine offered.

"That's right. And he and Linda would still have broken up. So in the end it won't make that much difference."

"No," Geraldine agreed. Stifling a yawn, she reached for the print-out lying on the bench in front of her, and ran her eyes down the results of the last scanner test Martin had run. To keep the conversation on its track, she made the occasional bland and undemurring noise. And in the end, as usual, her mother had talked herself out of her worries and round to other matters. "What about you and Robert, dear? How are things going with you?"

"The annual recruitment looms," said Geraldine. And knowing perfectly well how tedious her mother found the details of her job, she wasn't at all surprised when Mrs Carter swiftly changed tack. "And what about your yoga? Lulu says you've not been to class for weeks."

"No." Geraldine trawled for a lie. "Would you believe, in spite of everyone's protests, they changed the evening for the overnight experiments."

"To Friday? *Very* odd."

"Very."

"It seems a shame. Lulu thought that you really enjoyed those classes."

120

"I really did. How long will she be able to keep going herself?"

"I think she's been advised that at five months she should move on to some more gentle class."

"I might be able to go back myself round about then."

"That'll be good."

So the call ended. Robert, she knew, was outside in the corridor, chatting to Martin. He would be poking his head around the door at any moment and asking, "How did it go?" And yet the way in which the coming babies had been discussed had been so horrible that, rather as if it were some really unpleasant virus, she didn't want to pass it on — especially not to him. So when he asked, she only said, "That? Oh, it was a breeze."

He laughed. "I'm glad. Now you can save your self-control for the times when Lulu rings."

But even here, there was a happy reprieve. Though Geraldine did force herself to leave a couple of warm messages, the days rolled past with no real word from Lulu. It was a busy time of year, so they were grateful. Still, the remarks they made to one another, Geraldine couldn't help noticing, were gradually curdling from merely curious into sarcastic.

"At least we know that she's all right," Robert said out of the blue one day, when he was pulling a snapped lace out of the eyelets of his shoe. "Or she'd be crying on our necks again. Or asking for a loan."

"She's not done that yet, has she?"

He raised his head to stare. "You *know* she has. You lent her a packet that time she wanted to go off on holiday with that accountant fellow with the peculiar moustache. Did she ever pay us back?"

"Well, no."

"See. There you are." He went back to his task. "And what about the time that her electricity company was threatening to take her to court? You coughed up for that, too."

"I suppose I did. But that was ages ago."

"Not all that many ages. Mark my words, she'll soon be round here with the begging bowl. Wasn't it about now that she was dropping down to working only two days a week?"

"If the shop's even stayed open." Geraldine made a face. "Maybe if she needs money, she'll ask my mother first."

"Maybe she will. Maybe she already has."

What he said set Geraldine thinking. Just how close were Lulu and Jane? And just how secretive? She herself hadn't told her mother about the two big "loans" she'd given Lulu — or about all the other times she'd slid her stepsister money to keep her going to the end of the month. Perhaps the two of them would need a game plan now, otherwise they might both find themselves putting their hands in their pockets to pay the very same bills. Or one of them might end up nagging Lulu to make more effort to live responsibly within her income just as the other was resignedly spooning out cash.

Time to invite her mother to tea.

Jane came round on the Sunday. Robert stayed to be pleasant for a while, then made the usual excuse to vanish. "Bit of leftover paperwork, I'm afraid. Won't take a moment." Once he was gone, Geraldine let the conversation idle up and down several more easy-going avenues before she finally asked, "Mum, have you had a chance to *talk* to Lulu? Have you been able to ask how she and Harvey are ever going to manage?"

Her mother batted the question away. "I think they'll be all right, dear. After all, Harvey is barely a novice at this sort of thing."

"No, not the baby. I mean financially."

Mrs Carter looked shocked. "I'm not sure that's our business."

"It might be soon," suggested Geraldine, "if Lulu ends up having to wipe her baby's bum with nettles, and use it to beg in the streets."

It was quite clear that Mrs Carter hoped this topic could be abandoned. "Oh, things like this so often seem insuperable. Then they work out."

Geraldine pursued her point. "I'm sure he has a reasonable income. But a huge chunk of it is going to be chewed up by his commitments."

Mrs Carter said vaguely, "I always thought that Lulu had a very good deal with the rent for that flat of hers."

"I'm sure she does. But no doubt when she's dragging a toddler and a pushchair up those steps, she'll want to move. And he will still be paying out a load of cash to Linda."

"Oh, Geraldine! That isn't going to be for ever."

"Mum, Linda's *pregnant*. With his *third child*. Believe me, it'll be for long enough, or she would never have agreed to the divorce."

"I suppose you're right."

"I know I'm right. And you know that I'm right, as well."

Geraldine sat waiting. After a moment, Mrs Carter drew herself up in the chair. "Darling, I do wish you'd stop looking at me like that."

"Like what?"

"As if you thought it was my business to run Lulu's life. What can *I* do? I've tried my best to help her out since she was little. But she is not my child. I'm not responsible for her mistakes — or for what happens to her when she doesn't think ahead, or makes the wrong decisions."

Geraldine said carefully, "Mum, I'm not sure that you can really say that."

Her mother's response seemed to her almost testy. "I don't see why not."

"Because that isn't how it's been so far. Let's face it, it might not have been official, but you did pretty well adopt her into the family. And now she's in it."

Her mother's expression was impenetrable.

"*Isn't* she?" Geraldine persisted.

"Well, circumstances change."

"Perhaps they do," admitted Geraldine. "But this one hasn't changed much in the years since I left home. We still treat Lulu as if she's family. She still assumes she is. So we don't have much of a choice. When she and Harvey wake up and realize that they can't

124

manage, they're going to come to us. And you won't want to see her grovelling in the gutter. Neither will I."

"Lulu can get a job."

"Lulu has *never* had a sensible job. And that was *without* a baby."

Mrs Carter looked over at the clock. "Good Lord! Is that the time? I only really popped in for a moment. I should be going." She rooted in her handbag for her keys.

"Don't run away," said Geraldine. "Well, not before you've told me one small thing. In a few months, when Lulu comes round begging for a loan, are you going to give her money?"

Mrs Carter rose. "Geraldine, sometimes I feel you show a slightly off-putting inclination to be schoolmarm-ish. And you're being schoolmarmish now."

"I only want to *know*," said Geraldine.

"I really think it would be better if I left," said Mrs Carter. "Before I say anything I regret."

Geraldine caught her arm. "Now listen, Mum. This isn't anything to do with whether or not you *give* her money. I truly do not care. Give it, or don't. I simply want to *know*."

Jane Carter stared at her daughter. "But *why?* Why is it so important to you? It hasn't happened yet. It might not happen anyway. Lulu might find that staying home with a small child is really very tiresome. She might grow up and get a proper job. The two of them might manage perfectly well without my help. Or yours. So why are you getting so worked up about this business?"

"Because," snapped Geraldine, "all of my life, all I have ever wanted from you is to have some idea of where I stand! That's all! Is it too much? How does your own bloody daughter stand? And you will never tell me!"

There was a little silence while Mrs Carter stared unseeingly out of the window and Geraldine tried to regain her temper.

"Well," Mrs Carter said finally, "I certainly don't feel like being hectored. Especially on this topic. So I'll be off now." As she reached the door, she added with studious politeness, "Thanks for the tea, darling. And I will give you a ring next week, when both of us are in a slightly better mood."

"Ouch!" Robert said.

"Yes, ouch."

"You must have really got to her."

"She really got to me. Schoolmarmish! Am I really?"

"Of course not. I think it might be fair to say that you're the only member of your family who ever seems prepared to introduce a note of realism into a conversation. But schoolmarmish? No."

"You're *sure*?"

"Listen, she was just feeling under fire, so she lashed back. At heart, she probably feels as worried as you. I expect she's already envisaging watching her savings dribble out of her bank book across into Lulu's purse."

"Aren't we all?" Geraldine said sourly.

"Perhaps she'll think about it," Robert tried to comfort her. "Perhaps, by the time she phones next week, she will have realized that you're right and that it would be sensible for the two of you to have a joint game plan. In fact, I wouldn't be at all surprised if she phones earlier."

"She won't," said Geraldine, "because I criticized her. She can't bear criticism. That's why she couldn't live with my father. She doesn't put it that way to herself, of course. She simply calls him feckless. But that's what he always said. 'Your mother's very touchy, Geraldine. So maybe things are better with us in separate homes.' I didn't buy it at the time, of course. I just assumed that he was trying to cheer me up about us living hundreds of miles apart. But now I wonder. I mean, if every time he tried to say anything to her she froze up like she did today, why *should* the man have stayed?"

"To protect you?"

She laughed. "Come on! I didn't need protecting from my own mother."

"Maybe not way back then." He grinned. "But keep rattling her cage about her precious Lulu, and you might find you need an army on your side."

Her precious Lulu. All afternoon, as she was working through the recruitment files, she had to force herself to concentrate. *Her precious Lulu.* Geraldine would lift another application off the pile and find her mind was running in the past. The way her own achievements had been played down so Lulu wouldn't feel outshone. The way she'd get a sharp rebuke, but Lulu only ever seemed to get a sigh or tired headshake. Even the way that Geraldine had been forced to waste so much time scuffing her toes in the dirt outside the school and the library, the swimming pool and dentist, because, as it always turned out, "Lulu *insisted* that she wanted to come along with me to pick you up, but then it took a bit of time for her to find her shoes."

Her dad had laughed when she suggested that her mother liked Lulu better. She could remember him turning from where he'd been stuffing his bedroll away in the chipped melamine cupboard above the door of the tiny, strange-smelling caravan, and telling her. "Gerry, that's crazy. Of course your mother prefers you. You are her daughter!" She could remember saying sullenly, "It doesn't *look* like it." The caravan had rocked as he took those two steps to gather her in his arms. "Oh, sweetie, that's just because your mother's like one of those people who get a huge, aggressive dog and let it lunge and snarl and get in fights, but are too weak and sentimental to send it back. So they just go round making excuses for it. 'He's very gentle usually. It's just that he doesn't like black dogs.' "

She'd muttered into that awful old pullover of his that always stank of cigarettes and wood smoke. "The trouble is, I'm the black dog."

He'd pushed her backwards so he could inspect her face. "Sweetie, do you want to come to me? You know you can."

She could remember looking round his cramped, ungainly nest. How could she live on wheels, forever changing schools, going to Spain for a year here, France for a few months there? Eating his awful meals and sitting around with his weird foreign friends.

128

"No, thanks. I'd better carry on — at least till after the exams."

He was still trying hard. "Want me to speak to her?"

"No point." She didn't add that her mother was unlikely to take advice from someone she made no secret of regarding as having never grown up. "Oh, so he's off again, is he? Where is it this time?" she'd say each time Geraldine announced one of the frequent long hiatuses between visits. Indeed, the two of them were so accustomed to going months without a word from him that it had been quite easy for her mother to keep the news of his medical collapse from Geraldine until a couple of days after her finals, and act as if his death a few weeks after that would probably mean little more to his daughter than yet another long absence. Certainly, Geraldine thought sourly, she didn't remember getting the impression that she herself would ever have been able to use the death of her own father as the sort of lever that might get herself — as that tough cuckoo Lulu seemed to have managed so easily — into another family nest.

"Selfish!" Robert heard her muttering as he walked past her on the way to fetch more tea. "The selfish bloody woman! Running her life to suit herself the whole damn time."

"Lulu?" he asked her automatically, in case she wanted to lay aside her work and sound off for a while.

"No. Mum."

"Oh, right."

He nodded casually enough. But, inside, he was thinking it wasn't like him not to know, just from her tone of voice, which of the two she was thinking of when she came out with fierce little remarks like this: her mother or stepsister.

Something had changed.

CHAPTER
THIRTEEN

In fact it was only a few hours before Geraldine's mother rang to clear the air. "Dear, I've been thinking. And I should never have been so sharp with you. I realize that now."

Geraldine stopped struggling into the sleeves of her dressing gown and tried to reassure her. "No, honestly, Mum. I'm fine. You mustn't worry."

"No, dear. Please hear me out. Sometimes I really do forget what a great saint you've been, and how, however much poor Lulu gets on your nerves, you've always tried your level best to keep her interests at heart. I'm really sorry that I didn't want to listen to your worries. I realize they were all well meant."

"They were," said Geraldine. Deliberately, she started to make her case again, but this time sideways. "I mean, you know that up until now Robert and I have always managed to bail Lulu out with things like bills and holidays —"

"I didn't know that, dear. I didn't realize she borrows money from you."

"Oh, not that much," admitted Geraldine. "And not that often. Nothing we couldn't handle."

"Still . . ."

"But we can't subsidize her whole new family. And neither can you. So I just thought between the two of us we ought to make that clear right from the start."

She waited till her mother's silence prompted her to add, "That's if it *is* the start, of course."

"Oh, yes, I think so," Mrs Carter said a little too robustly. And then it seemed as if some urge towards honesty impelled her casually to add, "I mean, I've had to help her out a couple of times myself, of course."

"Recently?"

"*Fairly* recently."

"Not since the two of them moved in together, surely?"

"Well, as I mentioned, Harvey has not been having the easiest time of it himself."

Geraldine swallowed her irritation. "Well, all I think is that one or the other of us ought to be making it clear to Lulu that the gravy train has to stop here. I know it may sound mean and horrible. But she and Harvey will simply have to learn to live within their income."

Already her mother was dithering. "You're absolutely right. But I'm not sure it's the right time."

"It is *exactly* the right time."

"Oh, Geraldine! Really? What with the baby coming?"

"That is the point!"

"It seems a little harsh, dear. To tell her that you're going to cut her off just when she's probably going to need it most."

Geraldine glanced through the half-open door to Robert, in the bath. His knees were up. His reading glasses had misted over and slid down his nose. She loved him more than she could say. Simply the sight of him could make her braver than she'd ever been.

"Mum," Geraldine announced. "It's really hard to say this, but when I told you this morning that I didn't know where I stood, this is the sort of thing I meant. You tell me you agree with me that we should be firm with Lulu. And then, as soon as I say that we ought to act on it —"

"*Act* on it?"

"You know. By *warning* her. Then you back down and call me harsh and say it's the wrong time. So I don't know if we're in this together."

"It's not a battle, Geraldine. We're not on *sides*."

Geraldine tipped her head back and, staring at the ceiling, counted to three. Then she said quietly, "Please don't hang up the phone, Mum. Please just be kind, and listen. But we are back to what I was trying to tell you this morning. You say it's not a battle and we're not on sides. But sometimes I think it is. And you're on her side more than mine." Before her mother could break in to interrupt, she hurried on to explain. "Of *course* I tell myself that that is nonsense, and things only seem that way because Lulu's so hard to thwart, and so tempestuous that anyone in their right mind would do what they could to avoid ending up in a spat with her. But sometimes, Mum — like now — I know you know exactly how strongly I feel about things. No. More than that. I know you know not only how strongly I feel, but also that I'm right. And still you don't bother to take my side."

"Don't *bother*? Did I really hear you say, 'Don't bother'?"

"Yes, Mum. You did. Because that's how it seems to me. Things come to the crunch, and it's as if you know that if I lose out, I'll simply fade back into the wallpaper and there will be no trouble. But if you thwart Lulu, she will play her usual trick of going mental. So you just shrug and go her way."

"That is pure nonsense, Geraldine! You know that you're the most important person in my life! You always have been. All I was trying to do was point out that it's not going to be easy to tell the poor girl that, though she's pregnant, and though her job is being run down to nothing, and though the man she loves is being stripped of half his income, you and I are going to start acting tough."

Had Geraldine heard right? Were those her mother's actual words — "stripped of half his income"? Oh, hadn't one sturdy old feminist changed sides!

No point in quarrelling about that. Or anything, it seemed.

"I didn't say it would be *easy*," was all that Geraldine replied. "I simply said it should be *done*."

She couldn't wait to tell Robert. "You should have *listened*," she burst in to tell him. "If you'd been eavesdropping, you would have *growled*. She was astonishing. I'm trying to tell her how I feel, and she can't slide it back to poor, dear Lulu fast enough. But not the Lulu we know. Oh, no! This is some brand-new Lulu. Lulu, the Martyr Queen! And we must not on

134

any account be cruel to her because the poor lamb's pregnant, her job is being run down to nothing, and the man she loves is being 'stripped of half his income'. Can you *believe* it?"

"Hand me the towel. This bath is suddenly a whole lot less restful than I'd imagined. I might as well get out."

She handed him the towel. "I mean, why can't she tell it as it is? Why can't she speak the *truth*? Lulu is pregnant from choice. If, knowing what she knows about the shop, she hasn't bothered to find herself a better job, then that is her choice too. And it is Harvey's *responsibility* to support all four of his children."

"I couldn't drop these shorts into that laundry bin, could I?"

Obediently, Geraldine rose so he could lift the lid. She didn't stop. "Anyone would think his wife and kids were holding him at gunpoint, robbing him blind."

"You can sit down again now."

She sat down.

"No, you can't," he said. "I've changed my mind. I'm taking you to bed."

"I don't feel like it, thank you."

"Oh, I think you will."

"I won't. You know I won't. I can't just get in the mood."

"Oh yes, you can. You're always far more fun in bed when you're pissed off."

The scientist in her was quite intrigued. "Am I?"

He seized the moment and he dragged her off.

After, they lay together quietly, except for Puffer who was purring like a train on Robert's belly. "This is all getting out of hand," said Geraldine. "We start off with a simple plan to stop my stepsister crowing it over us because she's having a baby, and I end up hurling unforgivable accusations at my own mother."

"The things you said aren't unforgivable."

"They're pretty strong stuff. 'You never stand up for me.' 'You never make it clear that you're prepared to thwart Lulu in order to support me.' It isn't quite like telling her that she's got spinach on her teeth."

"You shouldn't worry about it. Your mother uses politeness as a shield to cover up emotion. I don't think it'll do her any harm to be reminded that you have feelings too."

"Still, I feel rather bad about pretty well turning the conversation into a bit of a threat."

"And maybe that will give her pause for thought next time Lulu is on the cadge. Or on the rampage."

Geraldine wasn't so sure. "Maybe. And maybe she'll tell Lulu how upset I got, and she'll crow anyway because she'll think I'm hiding my real feelings, and dumping all my pain and jealousy on Mum instead."

He turned to look at her. "Do *you* think that's what you're doing?"

She sounded certain enough. "No. No, I don't. I really believe the things I said. And, just this once, I said them."

"Twice, actually."

"Yes," Geraldine admitted. "Twice."

136

He chuckled. "At least now your mother can't be in any doubt about where you stand." He patted her hand on the coverlet. "And she's not going to say a thing to Lulu. There's nothing in that whole tirade that she'll want Lulu to know. So she'll keep quiet. Everything will roll along as if nothing's been said. I bet the next thing we get from your family will be a call from Lulu telling us Harvey is divorced."

"Or the quick flash of an engagement ring. Or floods of tears because he's changed his mind again and gone back to Linda."

"Oh, well," said Robert cheerfully. "Let's wait and see."

It wasn't any of those three. It was the most casual of calls from Lulu. "Geraldine! How's things?"

"Fine," Geraldine said. "Busy at work, as usual. But otherwise everything is tickety boo. How are things going with you?"

"Fine."

"Harvey's all right too?"

"In the pink."

"Good."

"Everything's swimming along," confided Lulu. "I was just thinking that I hadn't seen you for ages."

"No." Geraldine was tempted to add, "Not since the last time Harvey did a bunk," but in the end, of course, she just agreed. "No, not for ages."

"So I was thinking it would be nice to meet up. Do you remember the time we took Mum into Dunston."

"To see that play?"

"No, no. When Harvey and Robert came along as well. We all had lunch together."

"Oh, right. Well, nice idea. When did you have in mind?"

"Two weeks on Saturday? The twenty-fourth. Mum's free. She says she'll come."

Geraldine didn't need to glance at the calendar. All of that week was blocked out for recruitment. Final decisions were always made on the Saturday at a small lunch that she and Robert hosted. Once, all the arguing had gone on till four.

"Not a good day, I'm afraid. We're tied up through till tea time." She was about to offer another date, but Lulu had already broken in. "Shame! Oh, well. Never mind! I know what. Come round here in the evening after we're back, and have a drink."

Getting an invitation to Lulu's flat was so exceptional that Geraldine felt forced to accept. "We're going to be *shattered*," Robert grumbled later. "A whole day of Ivan arguing the toss for anyone who's mentioned Arsenal on their application form, and Grace getting testy if we don't choose all the women. Then having to pitch out to Lulu's! Oh, what a bloody day that's going to be."

"Some days *are* bloody. And there's still hope. After all, Harvey might have gone back to Linda by then. The evening might get cancelled."

"Some hope," said Robert gloomily. He took his irritation out on Puffer. "Hey! Off that counter! Now!"

"Is he stealing food again?"

"He is enormous," Robert said. "Fat as a barrel. I reckon someone else is feeding him."

"Apart from next door?"

"I wouldn't be surprised. We ought to follow him."

Geraldine laughed. "If you think I've got time to trail round after that cat all day just to see where he's scavenging . . ."

"No, no. I know that you're a busy lady." He grinned. "Can't even snatch a day in town with your own family. I'll take the role of sleuth upon myself."

CHAPTER
FOURTEEN

"Where is that little stripy hat?" Asked Robert, following Geraldine into the bedroom one evening, a few days later. "I thought, if we're not seeing them until the sixth, I might just post it."

Geraldine made a face. "Can't it wait? It's not as if she's had the baby yet. We've still got months to get it round to her place."

"Shows willing, though." He opened the closet doors. "Where did you put it?"

"Actually, I'm not sure."

He turned to stare at her. Then he sat on the bed and pulled her down beside him. "You're a liar."

"I'm not."

"You are. Come off it, Geraldine. I've known you since you were thirteen, and you have never yet misplaced a single thing. Not once. There isn't a cat's chance in hell that you have lost that hat. So tell the truth. Where are you hiding it? And why?"

Geraldine burst into tears. "Because I want to *keep* it, stupid!"

"Don't call me stupid. I have just been very clever and guessed your secret."

"I haven't *got* a secret."

"Oh, yes, you have." He gathered her to him. "That little hat's too nice for Lulu, isn't it? We want it for ourselves, in case the angel Gabriel comes to town, and gives us a miracle baby."

She flushed with shame. "It shouldn't *have* to be a miracle. There's nothing wrong with *you*."

"Or with you, so they said. It's just bad luck, or us together. Where is the hat?"

Dumbly, she pointed to the drawer in which he kept the climbing gear he hadn't used for years. Robert dropped to his knees and rooted through till he caught sight of all those cheery stripes, and pulled it out.

He fetched her hairbrush from the dressing table, and dropped the hat on top. "Look," he said. "Here is our little adopted child. Please, Geraldine. Look at his lovely bristles. Look at his pretty little wooden chin. Couldn't you love him? Couldn't you?"

"Her," Geraldine corrected through her snufflings. "Love *her*."

"That's settled, then." He whipped the hat off the brush and threw it on Geraldine's pillow. "We keep the hat, and we adopt something to fit it."

"We can't," wailed Geraldine. "You know they've only got older ones now. And ones with something wrong. And ones who've had a ghastly start in life. I couldn't do it."

"Then we'll go abroad and snatch a little brown or yellow one who matches the curtains." He saw her brave smile. "No, no. I'm serious. If other people can manage it, then why can't we?"

Her reason sounded so disgusting, even to her, she couldn't spit it out.

"It's Lulu, isn't it?" he said at last. "You are too decent to say it. But it's because if we start off adopting, Lulu will smirk."

Now she was howling her eyes out. "It's not the sort of thing you can keep secret. Before you can adopt, the social workers talk to *everyone*! They ask a million questions. They'd probably even want to talk to Lulu, and you can bet she would be mean enough to scupper it. She'd probably tell them that she thought I only wanted to adopt a child because I was jealous of her!"

She clung to him so tightly that her voice was muffled. His shirt front was already soaked. Her shoulders heaved. "She spoils *everything*! She always has! She always will!"

He took his chance. "You realize, if we moved abroad —"

"Oh, Robert!"

"No, don't 'Oh, Robert' me. Give me a reason — one stupid, silly little reason — why you and I should not pack up and leave this country tomorrow."

"We've been through this so many times!"

"So let's go through it once more. The house? That can be sold. The lab? They'll find replacements. People always do. Puffer? Well, he can go next door, or come with us. I'll make his options perfectly clear to him, and he can choose."

"Fine," Geraldine snapped. "But aren't you forgetting something? What about the real reason why it isn't quite so easy?"

142

He wasn't going to let concerns about his mother-in-law take over yet. He turned towards her, gripped her by the arms and peered into her swollen, tear-drenched face. "You'd like to, though."

"Oh, God!" said Geraldine. "If you only knew how much I'd love to get on a plane, order a gin and tonic, then look over my shoulder and say to the whole pack of them, 'Well, fuck you all!'"

How could their lives be held in place by such a short thread? He asked the question for the millionth time. "So tell me, why can't we give your mother a simple alternative? Stay here, or come. My parents did it, after all, and they're no older."

"They did it *years* ago."

"We can't run our whole lives keeping the path smooth for your mother while she spends most of hers making things easy for Lulu. That way that little bitch is running all of us."

"As usual."

But he'd heard something in her voice. Not just the usual hopelessness that came from feeling trapped. A streak of bitterness he might be able to use to lever out of her the thing he wanted so much. He took a giant risk. "Well, I have had *enough*. I know you want to go. If we don't get out soon, we will be all wrapped up in Lulu's problems with the baby. If we go now, we still have time to start again. So that's it, Geraldine. I am downloading the forms tonight. And I expect you to be standing there, holding your pen, ready to sign by bedtime. So where do you want to go?"

143

He waited. And he waited. And finally the words crept out.

"I don't care. *Anywhere*."

His heart thumped, but he took the greatest care to keep his voice as light as possible. "So. Only one criterion. A place where Lulu never smiled nor wept."

"That's about it," she admitted.

"Right, then," he said. "Leave it to me."

He held her till her eyes drooped shut, then slid his arm away and left the room, closing the door behind him so that the noise of the printer wouldn't wake her.

The moment he had gone, Geraldine's eyes snapped open. And till he came back with her supper on a tray nearly an hour later, she lay with her eyes fixed on the gleam of light leaking between the curtains, wondering how she would ever dare to pass this terrifying news on to her mother.

While he was out buying the food for their celebratory supper, Robert saw that the petrol gauge was halfway down. Enough for another week. But then they would be stuck into the interviews. Sometimes he lent the car to Jake to fetch the candidates who'd come by train.

Might as well fill up now.

While he was standing by the pump, he thought about the cars. They'd have to go, and his was only two years old. How much might they get for that? When he had filled the tank and pocketed more of the coupons that had invariably expired before his return to the garage, he moved his car to a space at the kerb beside the car wash, and walked round the building to the display rooms on the other side.

As he approached, the huge glass doors slid open sideways. Charging towards him, head down, was a little child. Robert stepped sharply to the left to stop him running out on to the forecourt. The boy dodged sideways, still trying to get past. Robert stepped back to cut him off again.

"Eddie!" he heard the boy's mother call. "Stop, Eddie! Come back here right now!"

Her angry shout did nothing more than galvanize the child into a more determined effort to escape. Now he was hurling himself from one side to the other, and practically bouncing off Robert's legs. Robert looked up to see what was keeping the mother from rushing over to collect her disobedient son. But every time he raised his eyes to glance round the showroom, the little terror charged again.

"Eddie! Come back at once!"

Ah, there she was, already hampered with another child. There seemed no chance of her getting a grip on both of them without assistance, so Robert reached down to scoop up the furious escapee. Holding him at arm's length to save his clothes from being scuffed by flailing shoes, he carried him over.

The mother was far too busy strapping the other struggling child into the double pushchair to lift her head. But she did say, "Thank you very much. Thank heavens you were there to stop him."

"No problem," Robert boasted. "After all, I am the England goalie."

Now she looked up. "You're not!"

"No," he agreed. "I'm not. But I was very good, you've got to admit. I certainly won that match."

"You certainly did." She turned to the child in the pushchair, who had begun a sort of uncommitted wail. "Oh, shut up, Barney!"

Robert inspected her. She was a pretty woman with huge dark circles round her eyes. Swivelling Eddie round, he pushed the grimly thrashing child into his side of the pushchair, then knelt to hold him firmly in place while she strapped him in too.

Then Robert rose. Should he say anything? Oh, what the hell. Why not?

"You're Linda, aren't you?"

He'd not just startled her, he realized. She looked quite scared. "It's quite all right," he said. "You're not supposed to know me. It's just that —"

Oh, now he was in trouble. How could he say, "It's just that my stepsister-in-law has stolen your husband"?

"It's just that I've met Harvey — very casually — a couple of times, and knew the twins were called Eddie and Barney. It was a guess really." He stuck his hand out. "Lucky guess, though, obviously."

She shook his hand. "Well, thank you —"

"Robert. I'm Robert Forsley."

"Robert. I'm very grateful. Those sorts of doors are really dangerous if you have kids." She looked at him a tiny bit more closely. "Do you?"

"Not yet," he said. "But we are hoping."

She gave him a warm smile. So that was settled. Good. A married man, not on the prowl. Filled with

146

matching good will, he said to her, "Why don't you let me drive you home?"

"You'll not have car seats for the kids," she said. But it was said so glumly he knew she wanted him to push. And so he pushed. "No problem, honestly. There are three straps in the back and you can sit between them while I drive very sensibly. It's only back streets and it isn't far."

Now she was back to looking just as anxious as before. "How do you know where I live?"

He thought it best to brazen this one out. After all, Harvey could bore on for hours with all his road routes and shortcuts, and she must know that. "I know because we've had more than one conversation about the best way to get through that part of town in rush hour, me and your husband."

"My ex-husband," she told him. "As of today."

"Really?"

"That's right."

She didn't sound upset. In fact, she'd said it lightly. So he felt he could ask, "What, the whole works?" and then persist: "Nisi and absolute, and all that legal stuff?"

"Totally!" she said. "The letter came this morning. Free as a bird. Why, I could even get married if I wanted."

The snort of contempt with which she followed this idea made it quite clear that nothing was further from her mind. He stepped into her place behind the double pushchair and, moving her aside, set off towards his car, somewhat surprised at how unwieldy the thing seemed to be with both boys in it. For some extraordinary reason, neither of the cantankerous pair made much of a fuss about being unstrapped and scrambling into his car, or having their seat belts fastened. Linda collapsed the pushchair, and as her coat fell open, he saw the thickening in her waist.

"Careful," he warned. "Don't even try to lift it."

She stepped back gratefully as he picked up the strangely folded contraption and dumped it in the boot. "Push their heads down if we go past any police cars," he warned. And maybe it was the mention of police that kept the two boys good as gold on the short ride. Barney was clearly playing with the bangles on his mother's arm, and, from the scratching sounds filtering over from the back seat, Eddie appeared to be making a stab at digging a hole in the upholstery. But they were quiet enough, and after checking the address with Linda, Robert felt relaxed enough to ask, "What were you doing in there, anyhow? Buying a car?"

"Trying to sell one of Harvey's."

"*One* of them? How many does the man have?"

Her voice was tart. "Well, two, it seems. The one he uses, and this other one he had the utter cheek to buy for his girlfriend."

Another news flash to take back to Geraldine: Harvey had bought Lulu's Renault!

He supposed Linda must have been watching his face in the mirror, because she added, "Yes, indeed! Quite a surprise! And I only learned about the bloody thing when we went through disclosure."

"Bloody!" shrieked Eddie. "Bloody, bloody, bloody!"

148

Barney joined in. Linda ignored the noise rising from either side of her, so Robert dared pitch his voice over the pandemonium to ask, "Is that the first you knew about your husband having a girlfriend? When you found out about the car?"

"God, no," said Linda. "I have known about Anna-Marie for *ages*."

"Anna-Marie?" said Robert. "Are you quite *sure*?"

CHAPTER
FIFTEEN

"Anna-Marie?" repeated Geraldine when Robert told her. "Are you quite *sure*?"

"That's what she said."

"You didn't dare ask what this woman looked like?"

"I know what you're thinking," said Robert. "But by the time we got to the house, Eddie had given up on digging through my upholstery to Australia and was asleep. She wouldn't let me wake him. She made me carry him into the house, and there on the kitchen table was a copy of the car's paperwork. Anna-Marie Larrien, and an address in Chester."

"Chester. Isn't that where Harvey generally goes mid-week?"

"That's right. He tends to start off on the A179, but if that's busy, then —"

"Oh, shut up! This is no time for jokes."

"Gosh, no!" he chuckled. "Not the time at all!"

Geraldine was still staring in astonishment. "Another girlfriend!"

"Yes. Oh, and there were a good few sneers about her baby-blue eyes and auburn curls and her French accent." Robert grinned. "I know that Lulu's capable of almost anything. But blue contact lenses and a wig? On top of papers in a false name for a secret car? No, I don't think so."

"Well! I am stunned. I'm absolutely *stunned*."

"It is amazing, isn't it? Still, it will give us more to talk about over our celebration supper."

"Celebration?"

"Have you forgotten already? This morning you agreed to leave all this and come with me across the world to start a whole new life."

She looked a little uneasy. His thumbs, round the champagne cork, stilled. "A problem, suddenly?"

"It's just this news."

"No," he insisted briskly. "All this has nothing to do with us."

He watched the tiny patches of pink rise on her cheeks. "Of course it does. This is my *sister*."

He didn't dare correct her. He knew that they were on the edge of something dangerous, and took a different tack. "Not quite the moment?"

"Not quite."

He slid the bottle back on the fridge shelf. "I think I'll have a beer, then."

It was quite obvious she wasn't listening. She was still standing staring into space. "Another mistress? I can hardly believe it. I mean, where does he even find the *time*?"

He felt his stirrings of anxiety gradually settle. It was a shock. Of course it was a shock. All she needed was to talk around the business for a little while, and get her bearings. Then they'd be back to where they'd been that morning. Halfway to free. Flipping the tab

151

of his beer can, he made an effort to immerse himself in this new episode of Lulu's life. "Well, after all, we know he wasn't home much. And he does have one of those jobs where you go spinning round the countryside, whining into your mobile phone about horrendous roadworks. I should have thought he could have run a dozen mistresses without much trouble."

"Do you think Lulu knows?"

"I doubt it. If he is sensible, he will have made sure that she's heard the *name*. But only as some sort of past entanglement."

Her voice was tart. "You seem to know an awful lot about this sort of deception."

He thought of snapping back. But sense prevailed. Instead, he started to unpack his groceries. "Well, I splashed out on oysters. So if we can't celebrate our plans to emigrate, we're going to have to have a rather nice bereavement supper for Lulu's hopes of a happy married life."

It was as well she wasn't listening. "Perhaps Linda's got the wrong end of the stick and Anna-Marie really is some long-gone entanglement."

He knocked this comfort on the head. "Geraldine, the car in question is even newer than mine. It's less than two years old. Lulu herself has been dating the man for longer than that." He couldn't help it. Shaking his head, he chuckled. "My, what a mess she's got herself in now. Oh, well! Thank God the two of us won't be around to have to pick up the pieces."

152

Geraldine flared up. "You just don't get it, do you? This changes everything."

He wasn't having it. Not this time. "Oh, no," he said. "It changes things for Lulu. But not for us."

"Of course it does! Do you suppose I can swan off with all this going on?"

He leaned across the table. "Why not? It's not our life. It's hers. And she knew Harvey was a liar and a cheat. We all did. After all, the man's been ratting on his wife for years and years. Christ, Geraldine! He even let his wife get pregnant while he was fucking Lulu! So don't tell me that this makes any difference to us, because it doesn't."

"Yes, it does."

"Why?" He banged the table right in front of her. "Why does it change things, Geraldine? Am I forever going to have to come a crappy second to your stepsister, and to your mum? Tell me. Just tell me." He put the boot in. "I'm only feeling the same way as you do about your mother, Geraldine. I only want to know whose bloody side you're on and where I stand!"

She stared at him. He made a childish face and, sweeping the bag of oysters off the kitchen table on to the floor, stormed out into the hall. Before she'd even risen to go after him, he'd grabbed his jacket and he'd left the house.

It was no more than an hour before he came home. "I'm sorry. I'm so sorry."

"Me too."

She had prepared the food. She'd left the oysters plain, the way he liked them, and had made an effort not just with the rack of lamb, but with the dish of layered potatoes that she'd guessed he'd had in mind. He didn't push his luck by pulling the champagne out of the fridge. Instead he found a bottle of wine.

"Where did you go?" she asked him while they were having their first drink.

"Down to the park," he said. "I spent the time kicking squirrels and spitting at the rabbits." And that reminded him. "Oh, by the way, on the way down there, guess who I saw strolling out of someone's door?"

She grinned. "Oh, please! Not Harvey?"

"Puffer! Can you believe it? That makes *three* places where he goes to stuff his big fat face. Three!"

"We could stop feeding him ourselves."

"I think we should. I doubt he'd even notice."

"I doubt he would." And then, at last, the two of them got down to the business in hand. "So," Geraldine began, "what are we going to say to Lulu? Anything? Or nothing?"

"Do you know," Robert said, "I really do believe that this might be the very first occasion on which the sensible thing to do might be to speak to your mother."

"Ask what she thinks?" Geraldine gave it some thought. "But you know exactly what will happen if I do that. First, just like me, she'll try to keep on thinking that this must be some mistake — some leftover thing to do with a previous girlfriend."

154

"Like what?"

She scoured her brain for something possible. "Like maybe this Anna-Marie did Harvey a big financial favour years ago when they were dating, and this car was a payback."

"Pretty unlikely."

"But *possible*. We all know Harvey gets himself into complicated situations. And if Mum can possibly keep thinking that things are still on track between him and Lulu, then she will."

"But you'll at least have told her."

"Yes, and she'll fret around it. I know she will. She'll work her way through a giant heap of innocent 'What ifs', and at the end she'll actually make a virtue of brushing the whole business aside."

"Whatever's easiest. Dependable old Jane!"

But Geraldine refused to smile. She was still thinking it through. "But Mum does like to *think* about herself as quite a caring person. So on the way to that decision she's bound to come out with reams of stuff about what a great support we'll all have to be to Lulu if things go wrong. And I will have to lie to her."

Ah, here they were again, back in the danger zone. "Oh, yes? Why so?"

"Because, if I don't, then I will have to warn her that she'll be on her own with all of that because we're making plans to leave."

He gave her an even look over his glass. "And the problem with that is . . .?"

She spread her hands. "I'm not sure I can do it."

His voice stayed a shade too steady for her comfort. "Not sure that you can do *which*, Geraldine? Tell your mother we're leaving? Or actually leave?"

She shook her head pathetically. "Not sure I even know that."

She'd never heard his voice sharpen so fast. "Well, do you know what I think, Geraldine? I think perhaps you'd better go round there pretty soon, so you find out."

Then, in an instant, he was back to his old self. Rising out of the chair, he smiled his usual easy smile and put out a hand to her. "On your feet, please. I think it's well past time for our nice supper."

She went round the following evening. On the drive over, Geraldine thought about how impossible it always seemed to be to get her mother to see anything from her point of view. Explaining to her about Harvey's perfidy would be a breeze compared with warning her that she and Robert planned to emigrate. She didn't fear that Jane would play the ageing mother card. She was too fit for that. More, that she'd seem impregnable. She wouldn't whine, or weep, or look outraged if Geraldine came out with her big news. She'd appear mystified, as if this quite extraordinary idea were being visited upon her in much the same way as Mary, the mother of the Lord, was given news from the angel.

And Geraldine would feel that she'd derailed her mother's innocent life. Was it unreasonable of a woman of Jane Carter's age to hope her only real daughter would stay on this side of the world? Was it unreasonable not to want to be left alone to pick up the pieces of Lulu's ever more tempestuous life? Her mother, Geraldine knew, would sit there with a baffled look upon her face — the same baffled look that Geraldine had always had to face whenever she had wanted to stray from any of her mother's expectations.

What could she say to soften the blow? Well, "You could come with us," obviously. And it would be sincere, for Robert wouldn't mind. But Geraldine knew already that Mrs Carter's eyes would simply widen just a fraction more, as if to remind her daughter that she was far too sensitive to voice the thoughts already rattling inside her head — thoughts no doubt along the lines of, "Sorry? Uproot myself at my age? Travel halfway across the world to a strange country, strange climate and strange ways?"

Somebody else's mother, Geraldine reflected, might actually *want* to go. Even if it was first suggested by a member of the family, it might become a true desire — easy to do.

But not Jane Carter. She lived her life her own way, always creating the impression that she was open and cooperative and more than willing to fit in. But every single thing she did suited herself. Everyone thought of her as the most agreeable companion. Still, she was the only woman in her book group the others never even asked to host the meeting. She was the only car owner in the bridge club not to commit herself to offering lifts to any other member. And, as Geraldine took care to remind herself as she turned down her mother's street, she was the only mother in the world who wouldn't have found some way of saving her own daughter from such a vicious cuckoo in the nest.

Why not? They'd gone through so many theories over the years. Robert once thought it was because, just for a year or two — the years in which Geraldine was conceived and born — her mother had been besotted with the hippy life. It was a world away from her own stiff-necked upbringing, and she had fallen into it with real abandon. Of course, once her baby was born, the idea had become a whole lot less appealing. Jane had flown home within the year, and then been eased into her own little house to save her parents' blushes. Pretty well every brief sighting of Geraldine's unkempt, chaotic father would have confirmed her in the path to which she'd chosen to return. But, Robert thought, maybe some vestige of fondness for that short, happy burst of gypsy life had stayed inside her. Maybe she thought that keeping Lulu — even the mayhem that surrounded the girl — was somehow romantic. Perhaps it fulfilled some hidden image of herself to which she didn't want to wave goodbye entirely.

That was the kindest of their suppositions. The others, after all, had to include pure wilful blindness to her own daughter's feelings, indifference or stupidity — and even spite. At the mere thought, Geraldine's stomach clenched, and after she'd swung the car safely into one of the tight little parking places behind the fire escape, her fingers still gripped the wheel. Even as she was knocking on the door, she realized that she didn't have the least idea how she would broach either the curious matter of Anna-Marie or the grim topic of their plans to leave.

Her mother seemed as pleased as usual to see her. "I'm glad you've come. I was just thinking what a shame it was you two won't be with us a week on Saturday."

"The trip to Dunston? We're sorry too. But it's the worst weekend. Everyone round at our house, squabbling over the new appointments. Half the recruiting committee haven't made time to read through the applications. The others either can't recall which candidate is which, or have the daftest reasons for wanting to hire or reject them."

"Never mind," Mrs Carter said. "At least I'll get to see you in the evening. And Lulu has suggested that since my birthday falls on the following Tuesday, perhaps we ought to celebrate that."

"Excellent plan. You don't want to miss another bridge night."

"I certainly don't."

It was the easiest start, and Geraldine found herself in no great hurry to spoil things. So, "Where are you having lunch in Dunstan?" she asked her mother.

Jane Carter shrugged. "Oh, Harvey's on about some place. The Frog and Sprocket, was it?"

"The Frog and Spanner. Where we went before."

"But you know Lulu. Once she starts dragging us around the shops, then it'll be wherever we fetch up. I think she wants to find some sort of neat little red-leather handbag."

While Geraldine suppressed the urge to mention how little use her stepsister was going to get out of that before she was reduced to hauling nappies round in sacks, Jane Carter jumped to her feet. "Speaking of neat little bags, dear . . ."

And she was off, into the bedroom. While she was gone, Geraldine looked round the room, trying to guess what she'd remember if she were half a world away. The chain of ivory elephants she'd always loved. The wonderful revolving bookcase they'd been forbidden to spin. The seascapes on the wall. And there, on the dresser, the photographs of Geraldine from a baby and Lulu from the age of eight. Geraldine rose from her chair to peer at them more closely. As if for the first time, she inspected her own solemn face. Then she looked over to Lulu's, brimming with guile and charm. Was *this* the quality her mother couldn't do without? Lulu's sheer wild indiscipline, and that force field of careless energy she carried round her? Did Mrs Carter, in comparison, find her own daughter leaden — as stolid and worthy as the tweed skirt that Geraldine had found herself unable to wear since Lulu spoke of it with such false admiration?

"There!"

It was her mother, back in the doorway with a small and garishly bright clip purse. "I found it at the bottom of a cupboard. I'm sure it used to belong to you. I was about to throw it out, but then I thought you might still want it. All these glass beads are very pretty. Do you remember it?"

Geraldine shook her head. "Not ringing any bells."

Nor should it. It would never have been Geraldine's. Not even way back in her teenage years would she have chosen something that cried out, "Look at me!" in such a Lulu-like way. A shaft of irritation ran through Geraldine. Where could it possibly have sprung from, this passion of her mother's to treat both girls as equals to the bitter end? Wouldn't she ever grasp that in order to do so she must stay blind for ever to her own daughter's nature?

Didn't her bloody mother know her *at all*?

She shook her head. "I've never seen that bag before. Give it to Lulu."

Jane Carter sighed. "She doesn't want it, dear. She said if you don't care for it, she might just keep it for the baby's dressing-up box."

"So you've already offered it to her?"

Even before the words were out, Geraldine regretted them. Oh, God! Oh, God! This was the stuff of childhood, this petty jealousy. As quickly as she could, she covered up. "Because I can quite easily drop it off at Lulu's place. We have a present for her baby anyhow, and we were planning to stop by."

And that was it. Her head was spinning, and she was exhausted. There was no way that she could tackle either the brand-new gossip about Anna-Marie, or Robert's fresh determination to leave the country. Geraldine sat quietly and let her mother talk about the felling of the trees along the lane into the park, and the new sign that had gone up outside the primary school, bragging about its "*Excellence in the Community*". "Yes, dear, spelled just like that! It actually makes me

161

want to *weep* every time I walk past." Geraldine kept her end up as best she could, and made great efforts to disguise her glances at the clock.

After an hour it was safe to leave.

"Enjoy your trip next Saturday! Have a good time!"

CHAPTER
SIXTEEN

Robert was amused. "So now we definitely have to take a present round to Lulu, or we'll be making a liar of her big, kind sister?"

"That is about the strength of it."

"Here, then." He fished under the bed, tugged out a bag and passed it over with a slightly sheepish look. Geraldine peered inside and pulled out a cotton baby suit covered in tiny yellow and brown giraffes.

She gave him a curious look. "Sweet," she admitted.

"But not *too* sweet."

"No, not like the stripy hat. Are we giving Lulu that as well?"

"What, give away our *baby*? You must be mad! Why do you think I went to all the trouble of getting this thing?"

She stared at him in wonder. Would there be *anything* that this man would not do to ease her life? Had he been put on earth for her alone? The baby suit was perfect. Sweet, but not too sweet. (She'd never cared much for giraffes.) She could imagine him slipping out of the laboratory while she was working in a closed experiment, and going from one shop to the next. She practically heard the echo of his voice as he told shop assistants, "No. Sorry. That's *too* perfect. I'm after something that looks nice, as if I took some care in choosing it. But it's important that it isn't anything that tugs the heartstrings."

"You are a gem," she said. "Truly you are."

"Can I come with you?" he begged. "I'd love to take a peek at how the two of them are getting on in that small flat."

She put on her stern look. "You promise you won't bring up Anna-Marie? Or tarty bead purses. Or anything at all that might put Lulu in a mood."

"Scout's honour."

He took a minute or two to follow her out to the car, and when he climbed in she saw he was clutching not just the wrapped gift but a glossy bag. "What have you got in there?"

"Champagne."

"You can't give that to them!"

"Why on earth not?"

"Because we're not supposed to know about the divorce."

"They'll tell us, surely. Then I can whip it out."

"Well, wait till he does. Then you can go downstairs and fetch it."

"Geraldine! It's three full flights of stairs!"

"Your choice," she said. "And anyway, Harvey might not be in the mood to celebrate."

Robert was grinning, she could tell. "Why not? Because divorce is so *routine*?"

She took her hand off the steering wheel to slap his knee. "No," she said sternly. "Because it's a failure and

164

a tragedy. And if we had to get divorced, and somebody brought round a bottle, I'm pretty sure I'd smash it over their head."

He sat tight, wondering about the way she'd put it. "If we had to get divorced . . ." Why "had to"? What was she thinking? That he might lose patience and go off to Australia without her? Had he been pushing her too hard? But if he didn't press her, they might go on this way for *ever*, all chewed up and spat out by Geraldine's small but very effective family.

What about half measures? Couldn't they move away? There was no rule, after all, that said you had to stay in the same town in which you had grown up. What if they moved to Cornwall? Or the Outer Hebrides?

Ridiculous idea. Just adding travel to trouble. Imagine Lulu coming for a week each time she had a major spat with Harvey, or fancied a spot of free help with childcare. Anyway, he didn't want to go to somewhere else in Britain. He wanted *out*.

They'd reached the block of flats where Lulu lived. It took an age of cruising round to find a place to park. "This is not going to be the easiest place to raise a child," Geraldine kept muttering.

"Her choice," said Robert, picking out the number of Lulu's flat on the security panel and pressing "Call".

It was Harvey who buzzed them in. "Come up! Come up! Lovely surprise!"

The flat was in the sort of mess Geraldine remembered from Lulu's teenage years: clothes strewn all over, dirty cups and plates piled on the coffee table and the floor, and shoes kicked off anywhere.

Harvey appeared impervious to the chaos. "Come in! Sit down!"

Robert sat on the sofa till Geraldine ordered him to rise so she could rescue the silk frock underneath. Folding it carefully and laying it over a chair arm, she started working her way along the sofa, picking up more stray clothes and adding them to her collection while Robert opened up civilities. "So, Lulu. How's it going, my sweet?"

"Tickety boo. The clinic says I'm dead on target with weight gain and baby size and everything."

"Congratulations!"

He let the word hang in the air, just in case Harvey took the chance to seize the moment to come out with his news. Unnerved by the silence that followed, Geraldine pitched in. "Honestly, Lu. You still look absolutely *ravishing*."

She watched her stepsister tuck her legs underneath her in that smoothly polished way that showed her pretty knees and long lean thighs to best advantage. "Thanks."

"We have a present." She tried her hardest not to say the next words, but she could not resist. "Mind if I clear a few of these plates away? Just to make room?"

"And keep the dried egg off the gift until the baby's seen it," Robert added lightly. And they were suddenly back into the old, old pattern. As Geraldine stacked plates and mugs and teaspoons, carrying them over to the cramped little kitchen area, Lulu pretended that she wasn't noticing, and took her time, displaying her scarlet fingernails as she picked at the wrapping paper, chatting the whole while.

Finally, finally, the little baby suit spilled out. "Divine! Oh, just divine!" She held it up, its little feet dangling above her knees. "Oh, Geraldine, I can't believe I'm going to be giving birth to something so sweet and tiny! Like a little bean sprout!"

"Did you hear that?" Harvey called over to where Geraldine was busying herself hanging stray tea towels on their hooks. "She says she's going to have a little bean sprout!" It was, thought Robert, rather as if he too had taken up the hobby of tormenting Geraldine.

"Talking of bean sprouts . . ." And while Harvey fetched the beer out of the fridge and put on the kettle, Robert went off on a riff about a brilliant Chinese restaurant he'd heard had opened in town. As Geraldine made Lulu's tea, the chat moved on, through restaurants to finding parking spaces, then to cars, and finally, as seamlessly as usual, on to the topic on which Harvey excelled. "If I were trying to find somewhere to park outside The Yellow Duck, I wouldn't actually approach through Tanner's Yard. I know it might sound mad, but what I'd do is . . ."

Blah, blah, blah, blah, thought Robert. He kept the look of asinine interest riveted to his face, but he was listening to noises from the kitchen area behind. Hadn't she finished yet? The dishwasher was loaded, the counters wiped, the coats back in the closet and all the stray shoes gone. Even the books and magazines were now in a tidy pile. Unless his wife was planning to drag out the vacuum cleaner and ask them all to raise their feet, then they could *go*.

She caught his next brief look and gave up scrubbing at the oven top. Harvey sensed movement. "Don't go. It's lovely having you. Time for another drink?"

"No, no," said Robert. "Have to get back. Tons of work this week and next."

"Shame!"

Though Lulu didn't rise, she did lift up her face for kisses, and Harvey saw them out. They clip-clopped down the stairs. Even after they heard the flat door close behind them they still didn't speak, for fear their words would echo up the stairwell. Only when they were safely back inside the car did Robert turn to his wife.

"Well, Flower? Enjoy your evening's skivvying?"

"*Somebody* had to do it."

He ticked her off. "Not true. You could have sat in it for half an hour. *They* always do."

She fought back. "Well, I much prefer sorting out mess to having to pretend that I am interested in where Harvey parks when he goes into town."

"It wasn't even where he parks! It's how he *gets* there."

"And she thinks that *we're* dull!"

They sat companionably through two sets of lights, and then he said it. "So. Not one damn word about his divorce."

"Not even when you said 'Congratulations!'"

"Not so much as a flicker. He is a master of deception, isn't he?"

"Just like her."

"Yes. Just like her." A thought struck Robert. "Maybe we're being unfair this time. Perhaps he doesn't know yet. Maybe there's been some mix-up in the post and Linda got her copy, but his went to the wrong address."

"No, no. He knows. They both know."

"And how come you're so sure?"

"Because I saw it."

It was a good thing Geraldine was driving. He would have crashed the car. "The notification of divorce? You *saw* it?"

"Yes. When I was taking all her clothes through to the bedroom. It was lying on the floor beside the bed."

"You actually read it?"

"I picked it up. My eyes fell on it, yes. I know exactly what it says."

"My God!" He stared at her. "What did you do?"

"The sensible thing. I put it back exactly where I found it and dropped the stuff I'd just picked up from all around it back on the floor. Then I came out."

"Do you suppose they'll guess you've seen it?"

Geraldine shrugged. "Who knows?"

"Well, well," he said. "At least we get another stab at drinking our own champagne."

"I told you divorce was not a matter for celebration," she reminded him.

"Sadly, in their case, the marriage will be cause for it even less."

They passed the first sign for the city centre. Suddenly Geraldine swung across into the inner lane. "Hey! I am *starving*. Want to go off to find that wonderful new Chinese restaurant that you were on about?"

"That? Oh, that doesn't exist. I made all that stuff up."

She turned to stare. "You made it up? But why?"

"Get them off all that soppy talk about 'sweet little bean sprouts'," he confessed to her.

Her face set. "Honestly. You mustn't think you're going to have to go through life protecting me from her. I know that I can take it."

"Maybe you can," he said. "But I'm afraid it's rather getting so I can't."

CHAPTER
SEVENTEEN

Tons of work, Robert had said. And it did seem as if the next two weeks were an appalling grind. Geraldine had a hard time raising her head from the pillow each morning, and by the early evening her yawns filled the room. "Can't we just pack it in? Can't we just *look* at the applicants and decide which look brightest?"

He shoved another heap of application forms along the table towards her. "Come on now, Geraldine! We know what happened last time they did that!"

Indeed, they did. One year they'd got the dates mixed up, and booked a holiday for the recruiting weeks. It took four years and one expensive court case to rid the firm of two of the incompetents the rest had hired. "How could you even *think* of giving that fool a job in this laboratory?" Geraldine had asked one of her colleagues after the trouble began. The answer beggared belief. "I thought the others would have read his stuff properly. And he seemed very plausible indeed during the interview."

It was the last time they would ever make that mistake! So on they ploughed, weeding out all the no-hopers and sorting the possibles into their various piles. It all spawned extra work, cross-checking unconvincing references and making phone calls. It took for ever. People could be so *cagey*. You practically had to stick a pin in some of them to get them even to begin to say anything doubtful. "Well, actually, I wouldn't claim that lab skills are her *greatest* strength . . ."

"What about setting up experiments? Is she any good at that? Does she think through the problems that might arise?"

"Well, here again, I suppose I'd have to admit . . ."

And on and on, while Geraldine or Robert ran a line through the poor girl's name and hoped she'd find a job somewhere where mistakes were less expensive. And less dangerous.

Then there was all the nagging that it took to make sure everyone on the appointments panel came in on the day of the interviews. But things did fall in place. For once, there were no train or air strikes, no sudden bouts of food poisoning, nobody phoning up from God knows where to say, "Oh, *Listbury*! I thought that you meant *Liston*." Everyone arrived on time. No one had lost their voice. And even the very shyest could be prevailed upon to speak up loud enough for George to hear. The two they'd shortlisted who lived abroad both managed to find a telephone that worked. And even more miraculously, so did the speaker phone on the committee table that caused such havoc the year before with all its whistles and shrieks. It was the longest day. "*How* many of them were there?" Anton demanded, pushing his photocopies of the application forms away from him across the table as they stood up to leave.

172

"Nine."

"Only nine? It seemed like *dozens*."

"Didn't it? I really liked that little guy from Sri Lanka. Who would have thought he'd be an Arsenal fan?"

"He probably isn't," Robert said drily. "He probably just did just as much research on us as we did on him."

"No, no," Jake countered. "No one but a real fan would know about that sideways header from —"

But they all cut him off, desperate to go their separate ways. "So," Geraldine reminded them, "choose your own favourites. Bullet point your reasons. And don't be late on Saturday."

"Saturday?"

And all the chivvying had to begin again. "No, *not* the thirty-first, Greg. This *coming* Saturday. The twenty-fourth." She watched poor Robert roll his eyes to heaven as he explained again. "And no, not here. Round at our house. The same as last year." She could have stuffed her fingers in her ears as, for the fiftieth time, he spooned out their address to someone who they'd always thought did have a brain. "Yes, I *know* nine o'clock is early for a weekend. But last year, if you recall, the arguing lasted for six hours. And Geraldine and I have to go out at seven to celebrate her mother's birthday."

To help him get them out of the door, she gathered up all Anton's annotated forms and shoved them into his arms. "You are supposed to take them home and think about them," she reminded him. "If you don't have a couple of favoured candidates, don't forget we will."

But everyone did, it seemed. All week her colleagues kept sidling out of doors and pulling her aside. "Remember that girl from Imperial? The one who researched under Tucker. Well, I was thinking . . ."

"That guy from Sri Lanka. What was his name? Bandaranaika? Well, I thought if we took him on, along with that fellow with the clumpy shoes . . ."

By Wednesday, Geraldine was sneaking out down the back stairs and standing for several seconds on the step, her head still in a spin, till she could even start to think about where she'd left the car. But they were getting towards the end of it. Complaints about the early start on Saturday were quietening down. Everyone admitted they had received the map link and the tip about the extra parking in the little cul de sac off Hawthorn Lane. If she knew all her colleagues, there would still be a few last calls from people trying to make a point before the meeting. "You know that applicant from MU? The one with floppy hair. Well, I want to make sure we take a really good look at him. I've just been going through a couple of the papers that he submitted. They really are quite excellent. *Excellent*."

"I certainly hope that lad from Enid Farley's lab in Chester gets a good look in. She doesn't tend to spoon out references as good as the one she's given him without good reason."

"Geraldine! Just thought you might like to take another peek at Lucy Fletcher's application forms before the meeting. I know she didn't come over that well in her interview. But if you look carefully at her academic record, I think you'll see —"

Finally, *finally*, they were on to the food. "So what's it to be?" asked Robert as soon as they got through the door on Thursday night. "Two entire evenings of slaving in the kitchen, or one big cheat?"

Geraldine pushed Puffer off the kitchen chair and dumped her bag in his place. "The same as usual. One big cheat. It's not as if they ever take the slightest interest in what they're eating, what with all the squabbling."

"Right, then." He dug for a coin. "Toss for who does the giant shop?"

"Fair enough. Heads."

It came down tails. "Heads it is," Robert said, slipping it back in his pocket. "But you will have to write the list."

It was enormous by the time she'd finished it. He used his coloured pens to introduce some order: drinks, bread, snacks and dips, salad stuff, quiches, puddings and dairy. Still, he knew it was going to be a marathon. "Go to that place beyond the garage," Geraldine suggested the following evening, as he was heading for the door. "At least they pack your bags." So he went there. And it was by the cheeses that he saw Linda for the second time, pushing the twins round in one of the deepest sorts of trolley, rather as if she had just picked the two of them off a shelf. Before she happened to look up, he took the chance to glance at her waistline. How fast did women in her condition spread?

Well, she was looking pregnant now.

All of her groceries were in a basket weighing down her arm. He couldn't bear to watch. "Hello," he said. "Remember me? Why don't you put all that stuff into the trolley?"

The look she shot at him was tinged with scorn. "What, so that Eddie can just hurl it out again on to the floor?"

"You could hurl Eddie out instead," Robert suggested. "In fact, you could make him push."

"Oh, he'd love that," said Linda. "You'd be less keen, though, the tenth time he banged the trolley wheels into your heels."

She seemed in no great hurry to peel away, so Robert prised the basket from her hand and held it for her while he asked, "How are things going, anyway?"

"Not bad," admitted Linda. "I must be honest and admit that watching Harvey muck up his whole life somewhere else is proving a lot less stressful than living with him while he ruins mine." She reached for butter. "And it's a lot more fun."

"Fun?"

"Yes." She gave the twins a cursory glance, as if to check they weren't yet old enough to get the drift of what she was about to say about their father. "You know he's got *another* girlfriend now?"

"Well," Robert said, "I must say, as it happens, I —"

She didn't stop to hear the rest of his confession. "Another girlfriend! Can you believe it? And guess who told me!" Clearly, again, she didn't expect an answer. "Anna-Marie! That girl he gave the car to."

"Really?"

"It's unbelievable, isn't it? The woman arrived on my doorstep last week. She actually had the nerve to stand there and weep and wail in front of me. In front of me! His former *wife*!"

She had been happy enough to label Harvey's behaviour as amusing, but clearly the mere thought of the visit from Anna-Marie caused outrage.

"That's very French," admitted Robert soothingly. "Unless, of course, all she was after was repairs to the car."

It worked. Immediately Linda was back to laughing. "That would have made more sense. I would have respected her more. But, no. She simply kept snivelling on and on about this other woman who had stolen Harvey." She brushed aside the fingers he hadn't noticed creeping into the basket that he was holding. "Get off, Eddie! If you rip through that packaging, the macaroni will spill on the floor."

Robert moved out of Eddie's reach. "Another woman, eh?"

"Yes. And guess her name! Just guess!"

He could play Rumpelstiltskin and astonish her by coming out with it. But in the end he put aside temptation and just said, "What?"

"Lulu!" She hooted. "Can you believe it? Lulu! The perfect name for someone's tart. I almost had to laugh. Anna-Marie got quite cross. I think she'd made the big mistake of coming round in the hope that the two of us might become sisters in grief." She grinned. "I put her straight on that. 'Don't look to me for any tears,' I told her. 'I'm thrilled to be out of it.'"

She broke off, anxious at the unusual absence of trouble from inside the trolley. But Barney appeared to be doing nothing more tiresome than making a nest among the shopping bags she'd brought along, and Eddie was busy shooting at passing customers with a pilfered carrot.

Her face turned grave. "I feel like someone getting out of jail," she said. "I'm certainly not going to hang around weeping for that louse."

He felt a rush of warmth for her. He knew that if she had only been what she supposed she was — a perfect stranger — he would have dared invite her round for supper. Perhaps because he and Geraldine had been together all through school and university — and now again in the lab — they'd never made enough friends. And none of the few they had lived very close by. It would be such a pleasure to have this merry and outspoken woman round for a meal. But how on earth could it be done? The minute he admitted that Lulu was part of his extended family, she would feel cheated — as if, just like her creep of an ex-husband, he too had somehow been deceiving her right from the start.

"You're absolutely right," he told her. "You're still young. And very beautiful. And you don't even have to worry any more about having children."

"Indeed I don't," she said, patting her stomach. "I really, really don't!"

He did the very best he could to act astonished. "You're not . . . ?"

"I am! I am! Five bloody months!"

"Jesus!"

She grinned again. "I don't mind. Honestly, I take the line the more the merrier when it comes to families."

"Still, the expense!"

She looked a bit embarrassed. "Well, actually, that's not so much of a problem as it might have been. My family were never very keen on Harvey. So they did tend to keep the two of us on quite a tight leash."

He was a bit at sea. "In which respect?"

"Money." She shrugged. "Well, handouts, really, I suppose you ought to call them. They're quite well off, my mum and dad. Did Harvey never mention it? He seemed to me to moan about it quite a lot." She caught his baffled look. "About the way the easy money vanished when we got married." To put a stop to Eddie's renewed wailing, she bobbed down for the carrot he had dropped. "But now he's gone, they're being wonderful again. Wonderful!"

"So," he said, "happy ending, after all. You're free. And you're not broke."

"That's right."

Again, he felt that rush of warmth. "I am *delighted* for you. You can do anything you want."

She beamed at him as if he were an angel come to dispense even more tidings of joy. "That is exactly what I'm going to do," she said. "I've made my plans. As soon as our paperwork comes through, the boys and I are off to stay with my brother and his wife and their four children. Just till we find a place of our own, of course!"

"Where?" Robert asked, although he rather feared he knew already.

She was ecstatic still. "Australia! Lovely Australia! And a whole new life!"

He felt it like a body blow. And took it for a sign. Grimly he wheeled his trolley up and down the aisles, throwing in everything from the list that he could see and tossing in alternatives to things he couldn't find without a moment's thought. He waited impatiently while all his groceries went through the check-out and then piled everything carelessly in the car. The moment the radio sprang into life, he reached to turn it off and drove home in silence. The moment he'd dumped all seven of the massive bags on to the kitchen table, he disappeared upstairs.

"Hey!" Geraldine called after him. "Are you going to help me unpack?"

He just pretended that he hadn't heard. When he came back down he was carrying the forms he'd printed out so long before.

"Sign here."

She looked up from the bag she was unloading. "Sorry?"

Making a space on the table, he flattened one of the sheets of paper in front of her. "Just what I said. Sign here."

She wasn't even looking at the pen, let alone reaching for it. "What are you on about?"

"Forms," he said. "This is your application form to emigrate. If you don't sign it, I'm not going to do a single thing about this lunch."

"Don't be ridiculous. I know you've just done the most enormous shop, but —"

"I mean it, Geraldine. If you don't sign, I'm going to leave the whole damn lot to you."

She laughed. "This isn't funny. You can't barter going to Australia with making lunch for thirteen."

"Fourteen. I have invited Puffer. And yes, I can. And am. If you don't sign this paper, I'm not even going to unpack the beer and stack it in the fridge."

"Oh, Robert! For God's sake! Don't you think that the two of us have got enough to get through?"

"Sign, then."

"Stupid!" She turned her back on him and delved inside the nearest bag. Out came a carton of eggs. She shoved it on the table, and dived in again. This time it was a head of celery. She put it on the table. "See. I can do this all by myself."

"Go on, then."

Once more she dug inside the bag. Out came a punnet of tiny cherry tomatoes. But she was holding it in the wrong place. They started spilling out, and as she moved to catch the other corner of the punnet, her elbow hit the head of celery and rolled it over, knocking the egg carton off the edge of the table.

All the eggs had fallen out before it hit the floor.

"Oh, shit! Oh, shit!"

"See. There you go. Now sign the paper, Geraldine, and I will unpack all the groceries all by myself. And clear up that mess. And get more eggs. *And* make you a cup of tea into the bargain."

She shook her head at him. "You're mad," she told him. "You do realize that you are off your head. Because I can sign that form easily enough. But you can't actually force me to emigrate. You do know that?"

"Of *course* I know that."

"You just want me to sign? I mean, you promise you're not planning to dope me and smuggle me out of the country in a body bag, or anything?"

"Would I do that?"

"How should I know? You've clearly gone bananas." She turned away, and found herself stepping in the broken eggs. "Oh, bugger! Now the damn stuff is on my shoes! What next, for God's sake?"

"The ice cream," he warned. "It's melting. And the cheesecake's going soft around the edges. You'd better sign this form — unless, that is, you want to go out shopping."

"You're bats," she told him. "Absolutely *bats*. A signature under duress means nothing."

He put the pen into her hand and folded her fingers round it. "It means a lot to me. So sign."

"All right," she said. "But only because I really, really fancy a cup of tea."

She signed her name. He leaned down to inspect it carefully in case she'd written Mickey Mouse. And then he sent her off into the living room to watch a film while he unloaded all the groceries, cleared up the egg mess on the floor, and started planning.

All the while, in the background, she could hear the same particular snatch of song filtering in through the doorway.

"What's that you're warbling?" she finally called through.

He popped his head around the door. "Swing Low, Sweet Chariot," he lied. And she said nothing, though the two of them knew perfectly well that it had been "Waltzing Matilda".

CHAPTER
EIGHTEEN

He told her next morning as she was reaching for the cup of tea he'd put on her bedside table. "While I was in the supermarket yesterday, guess who I saw."

She banked her pillows up as usual, and stared at him as he explained that he'd met Linda again. Even before he'd properly embarked on the story, she had cut in. "No, no. Slow down! I want a really full account. Don't miss a single thing."

Obediently he ran through the conversation, telling her everything, right down to Barney's nesting in the heap of bags, and Eddie's carrot gun. Geraldine sat entranced, like a child hearing a fairy tale. "Who would *believe* it?" she murmured in sheer wonder when he had finished. "Absolutely amazing. An ex-wife who can't wait to vanish tidily from the scene, and two nubile mistresses who actually seem to want to carry on with the creep, even though they know what he's like." She shivered with impure delight. Then her face dropped. "Mind you, poor Lulu!"

But he'd been thinking about that. He shook his head. "In my view, Lulu has been really lucky."

"*Lucky?*"

But he was glancing at the bedside clock. "Look, sweet-pea, hadn't we better be getting up?"

She waved a hand. "They won't be here till nine."

"Still. Lots to do . . ."

Sighing, she pushed back the covers on her side. "Oh, I suppose you're right." As usual, she acted casually enough, but managed to slide past while he was still unbuttoning his pyjamas, beating him to the shower. Emerging a couple of minutes later, she asked again, "Why did you say you thought that Lulu was lucky?"

He stepped into her steam and called back over the partition top. "Well, look at it from her point of view. Who do you think that Lulu would rather have snapping away at Harvey's heels? Some cast-off mistress who can be easily frozen out? Or an impoverished ex-wife trying to prise child-support money out of him for the next fifteen years? Personally, I think anyone sane would jump at the mistress."

"Jump *on*, more like, if we know Harvey," Geraldine said cheerfully.

He stumbled out of the shower and knotted a towel around his waist. "Well, I think they both probably know that even with Anna-Marie popping out of the woodwork they haven't done too badly. He can't earn *that* much, after all. He must be thanking his lucky stars that his ex-wife is back in her rich parents' good books."

"That's if he knows."

"Yes. If he knows."

When she was dressed, Geraldine followed Robert down to the kitchen, where he'd already buttered a slice of toast for her, and was now pulling boxes and trays out of the fridge and the freezer. "Better slice up these tarts and quiches and stuff so they'll defrost quicker."

"I'll do it." She reached for the knife while he got rid of all the packaging. They worked companionably for a while, both drinking tea. "Good thing we're only going for a drink tonight," he said after a minute. "By the time we get round to Lulu's, we're going to be sick of food."

His mention of the coming evening sent her thoughts down that track. "It's really awkward, isn't it? Knowing all this stuff, but not having any idea at all who else knows what."

"I rather like it," he couldn't help admitting. "Gives me the feeling of being the puppet-master." He caught her baffled look. "You know. Like looking down and seeing people acting parts and saying things they don't believe." He leaned across to peer at her handiwork. "What *are* you doing?"

"What does it look like? Slicing things up."

"But they're all any which way."

"No, they are not. I just have large and small slices. Different people prefer differently sized portions."

"But it looks *mad* like that. Why didn't you cut all the large ones on one side and all the small on the other?"

"Because people always feel obliged to keep tidy as they go around. This way, there's always a choice of small or large serving next." She pushed him further away from her, back to his own task, and carried on with what was on her mind. "But it's so easy to put your foot in it. Look at tonight. I know it's Mum's birthday we're supposed to be going there to celebrate. But it'll be quite hard to get through the whole evening without a load of talk about Harvey and Lulu's future."

"You mean, not being sure if Lulu knows yet about Anna-Marie?"

"Or if Harvey realizes his wife is planning to take all three of his kids so far across the world that he won't be able to visit them without spending a fortune."

"And having Lulu kick up a storm because he's using up his holiday allowance."

"And because she's being left alone for weeks on end with a small child." She couldn't help but shudder. "My God, divorce is bloody."

"It certainly does seem to be when there are children involved."

Why did his carefully qualified reply unnerve her so? It was a sensible remark — one that he could have made at any time over the last twelve years without her thinking twice. But when she glanced his way, she could see nothing in his face to hint at a hidden meaning, so she distracted herself from her unease by picking up the conversation where they had left it. "I don't suppose that Harvey will even think of going that often. After all, so far he hasn't shown himself to be the sort of father who worries much about the future of his children." She shrugged. "In fact, from what you've said, it sounds as if they will be better off out there with sensible Linda and all her family. If they're as well-heeled as she has made out, she can afford to take trips back as often as she wants. And let them come alone, when they get older."

Robert was silent.

"Don't you think?" she prompted.

He laid the garlic press down on the counter and turned towards her. "I don't know. I still feel uncomfortable."

"You said you quite liked being puppet-master."

"Not about this," he admitted. "I have no time for Harvey. You know that. But I think I will feel just terrible if we find out all this is happening behind his back, and yet say nothing."

"Harvey is barely entitled to complain about things going on behind *his* back."

"But this is different," Robert said. He sounded almost cross. "This is his *children*. He might have been a hopeless husband and an undependable lover, but we've no reason to believe he doesn't love his kids."

"What are you saying? That you think people have no chance at all of being happy if someone they love moves halfway across the world?"

He looked up to find she was watching him. Test question, was it? Coolly, he looked her in the eye, and smiled. "Oh, Geraldine, I thought the interviews were over earlier in the week."

She waited. But no answer came.

Then the phone rang.

It was the start of a series of calls. "*What* time did we agree?"

"You did say *left* after the roundabout?"

"You have remembered I'm a vegetarian, haven't you? And that includes fish, I'm afraid."

"You won't be horribly offended if I bring my own coffee? You see —"

Robert put down the phone for the fourth time. "I think we're home and dry. That's at least half of them who have remembered it's today."

She clattered the last of the coffee cups on to a tray. "We won't be home and dry till we have all the names we want on the final list, and none we don't."

He glanced at the top of the cupboard where he had hidden the form he'd forced her into signing the night before. He almost dared to say, "It matters that much, does it? You still plan to stay?" But it was not the time to get into a wrangle about their future. In any case, one of the things he'd always loved about his wife was her sheer fairness, her determination to get the world around her ordered so that, wherever possible, people got what they deserved. If she were handing in her notice on the very next day, she'd still fight tooth and nail for the best candidates.

Even now she was fretting, staring at the master list on top of the pile of papers. "Want to run through the game plan one more time?"

"Relax!" he said. "I could go through it in my sleep. Miller and Bandaranaika for certain. Then Chang and Fletcher by preference."

"And Rosen if we're on a winning streak. But most of all, we have to head off the weak reeds."

"Sendar and Scott. I know."

They both got back to work, counting out cutlery and glasses, finding more serving spoons and rinsing out the jugs. The door bell rang. Once again, Robert glanced at his watch. "Can't they get anything right? This one is twenty minutes early!"

"Maybe it's something else."

But she was wrong. It was the first of their colleagues standing on the doorstep. "Martin! You're well in time."

He slid in sideways, like a police officer entering a room in which he suspected someone might have a weapon. "Actually, I was hoping to have a quiet word before the others arrive."

"We're all ears," Robert said. "Happy to share in any confidence going about the bunch that we're discussing today."

"Well, that's the point," said Martin. "You see, the thing is —"

The phone rang. "Just a tick," said Robert. "That'll be someone checking the address. Just let me get it, will you?"

While he was taking the call, Martin moved closer to Geraldine. Staring morosely at the cheese and broccoli quiche in front of him on the counter, he said in the most accusing way, "You *seen* your shares?"

"Yes, thank you." Not wanting to be baited yet again for the eccentric way in which she chose to divide things, Geraldine stepped aside to switch on the kettle. "Coffee?" Even before the noise of beans being ground had died away and she could hear again, Robert was back. "So, Martin. What were you wanting to talk about?"

Again the phone started up. "Look, can you leave that?" Martin said. "I mean, I really need —"

"Better not," Robert interrupted. "It's very close to nine now. Someone might be lost."

"Want to tell me?" said Geraldine, while Robert rushed off again.

"Might as well wait," said Martin. "Surely he'll only be a moment."

And he was. While Geraldine poured scalding water into the coffee jug, Robert clattered in the cupboard. "I'm sure that I bought biscuits, Geraldine."

"Look —"

"You did," said Geraldine. "I put them way up with the cake tins."

"Why?"

"So that I have to fetch a stool each time I want one."

"But I bought ones you don't like."

"I know," said Geraldine. "The problem is that suddenly I don't appear to mind them quite so much."

"Have they all *gone*?"

Martin stepped forward. "Look —"

Robert spoke over Martin's interruption. "You've actually scoffed two entire packets of chocolate ginger biscuits?"

"Be quiet, both of you," said Martin. "This is important! I think you ought to know —"

Just as they turned to look at him, the doorbell rang.

"I'm sorry." Robert made a face. "Give us just one quick moment to set whoever this is up with some coffee. I promise you, as soon as someone else turns up,

Geraldine and I will sneak away into the other room to hear whatever it is you want to tell us."

But the chance never came. One after another everyone spilled through the doorway, begging for tea or coffee. Jake even asked for toast. "Well, I thought, rather than be *late* . . ."

The others picked up the theme. "Yes, since we're all here now . . ."

"Might as well get stuck in."

"The sooner we start . . ."

They took their places around the table. Pulling his own chair back, Robert tried offering Martin one more apologetic shrug. But he was staring moodily down at the table. Geraldine gave a brief résumé of each candidate's strengths and weaknesses before she let the discussion roam. Whenever possible, she left the talking-up of all her favourites to other people before beginning to corral and quantify the views round the table. And things went well. Though Martin made a point of staying in his sombre mood, staring down at his papers and saying nothing, all the discussions went the right way, with people being far more sensible than Geraldine had hoped. More than once, Robert winked at her across the table as, first, the candidates they favoured crept up the list, then Sendar and Scott were each in turn sent packing.

The next time Geraldine drew a sheaf of papers towards her, the others groaned. "Coffee break, please!"

"Ten minutes, Geraldine. That's all I ask."

"What do they call it in America? Comfort break, is it?"

Robert stood up. "Who is for coffee and who for tea?"

"I'll help you." Instantly Martin was out of his blue study and on his feet. Following Robert out, he caught his arm. "Listen," he said, "I have to ask you. Have you seen our shares?"

"What shares?"

"What shares?" Martin was staring. "Only the shares that you were given when you joined the company."

"Oh, those." Robert reached for the kettle. "I don't pay much attention. There weren't that many, and I've never bought or sold them since." He raised his voice against the gushing of the tap. "Why? What about them?"

"Yesterday they went haywire. I think that something big is in the offing."

"Something big?"

"You know," said Martin. "Some sort of takeover."

"Another pharmaceutical? What, like Delwort and Price?"

"I'd have thought so."

Robert shifted the milk and the sugar bowl closer together so he could fit more mugs on to the tray. "Would that be bad? I mean, have you been buying more and more over the years? Are you at risk financially?"

"Do get things straight," said Martin. "The share price is going *up*."

"So what's the problem?"

"The *future*, Robert! Just the bloody *future*! We are the smallest company in the group. We cost a lot to run, and we are stuck away out here, miles from the others. If Delwort and Price begin to rationalize, they're bound to start with us."

"Meaning?"

"The usual, of course. No more recruitment. Lots of redundancies. Move south or go. That sort of thing." He nodded to the door he had pulled shut between the two of them and all the others. "That's why I wanted to talk to you and Geraldine before the meeting. I'm really not sure this is fair, choosing the finest people and offering them a job that will almost certainly go down the drain in months." He spread his hands. "It's fine for me. I'm practically retirement age already. I'd be quite glad to snatch some cheque for redundancy and swan off into the blue."

Now Robert had stopped pouring, and turned to look.

Martin passed him the lid to the coffee jug. "But what about all these young hopefuls we've been talking about this morning?"

"You haven't said a thing," Robert accused him. "You've just been sitting there. You didn't even speak up for Bandaranaika."

"Indeed I didn't. How would you like to move yourself and your family across the world for a new job and find it crumbling beneath you within a year?" He scowled. "No. I think the poor buggers should be warned, before they turn down any of their other chances to make the serious mistake of coming to us."

He absent-mindedly picked up a biscuit and broke it in half. "And, to be frank, I rather thought that Geraldine would show a little more concern."

"Geraldine?"

"Yes." Martin stared at the biscuit halves as if he couldn't think how they had ended up between his fingers. "I mean, before the meeting, I asked her if she'd noticed how the share price had started shooting up. She said she had, but I must say she didn't seem too bothered."

"She knew the share price? *Geraldine?*"

"That's what she said."

Robert picked up the tray. "Listen," he said. "Family celebration tonight. Not a free minute. But I will promise you this. Whatever everyone decides today, we won't let anyone send out job offers. We will sit on the list until the three of us have had a chance to talk again."

"There's a good fellow."

"Open the door for me, will you?"

"Righty ho."

And it was with a lighter step that not just one of them, but both, went back to join the others.

When they'd all gone, Robert asked Geraldine, "*What* was it Martin said to you?"

She clattered more of the dishes into the sink. "As far as I can make out, Martin barely said a word. It seemed to me that he was in a mood from start to finish."

"I mean before," said Robert. "In the kitchen. When he first came, while we were setting up."

"Nothing," she said again. "He just said something scathing about my kitchen skills."

"Really?" Robert was curious enough to be waylaid. "And what was that?"

"Just pitching in to criticize the way I cut the quiche."

"What did he say *exactly*?"

"I can't remember. Something like, 'Look at your awful slicing.'" At leisure for the first time since the morning to feel outraged, she scowled. "Rude man. Sulking all day."

Robert had turned away to hide his smile. "It couldn't have been, 'Look at your *shares*,' could it?"

"I suppose so. Why?" She looked at the clock. "No, don't tell me now. Don't even speak to me. If I don't concentrate and get a move on, we're going to be so late that Mum will huff and puff, and Lulu will play her usual trick of pretending she thinks we've had a quarrel."

"Nice to have someone so predictable in the family," he told her happily.

But she had gone.

CHAPTER
NINETEEN

The moment they were through the door he sensed that something significant was in the air. Though it was Lulu's flat, Jane Carter was the one who let them in, and it was obvious from her stiff and unnatural smile that she was steeped in unease.

Something had happened. Something that wasn't welcome. And Lulu wasn't in the room. Could it be possible that she was losing the baby? Greeting his mother-in-law as quickly and efficiently as he could, Robert moved past in search of Harvey. But he was standing calmly in the tiny kitchen area, looking as amiable and vague and well-intentioned as ever.

So, not the baby. But something else. Instinctively, Robert moved closer to Geraldine and laid a hand on her back as Lulu suddenly appeared, framed in the bedroom doorway. It was a proper entrance she was making, standing there radiant, like some great Edwardian actress soaking up rays of admiration from her besotted audience before moving into her role. "So there you are!" she cried, all warmth and welcome. "I was just starting to worry."

"No need," said Robert.

He looked around, already on the hunt for clues. The flat was clean, and tidier than he had ever seen it. It looked quite different — like a fresh setting for whatever part it was that Lulu had decided to play. Simply to put a crimp in her performance he turned to Jane, who was now sitting primly on the sofa, and held out the bottle they had brought with them. "So! Happy birthday for Tuesday! Many happy returns! Your health and happiness."

"Well, thank you, Robert." And yet she didn't seem to want to take the cheerfully wrapped bottle. Her hands stayed in her lap. So Robert swung around to hand it to Harvey. "Here you are. This time we actually remembered to chill it."

"Yes, happy birthday, Mum," Geraldine echoed. She turned to Lulu. "And you are looking as wonderful as before. More so, in fact."

Lulu was twinkling. "I don't know, really I don't. I keep on willing the whole business along, but still don't seem to have the gift that other people have of getting fatter."

She let the idiotic complaint die in the air as she pretended to hide a glance at the loose top that Geraldine was wearing. Now Robert pressed his hand even more firmly against his wife's back as a warning not to rise to the bait. And she responded cheerfully enough, "I know! I know! No need to tease. It's been the worst two weeks. All of the usual problems with this year's recruiting, and now it seems some other complication has come up to do with the firm's future."

Since no one pressed her to explain, she finished lamely, "So I've been eating tons and tons of biscuits."

Politely, Lulu left the "and-doesn't-it-*show*" look on her face for only a moment before saying, "Never mind. No biscuits here tonight. Only *champagne!*"

Again that sparkling look — almost of triumph. Who would crack first? No point in trying to read Harvey's face. The sheer self-satisfaction of the man made his expression impregnable. How about Jane?

"So," Robert turned to her. "Have a nice day? What did you do in Dunston?"

She squirmed. She absolutely squirmed. There was no doubt about it.

"My Lord!" she said. "The canapés! I put some in to warm, but Lulu's stove is a real nightmare. Just let me check they're not ruined."

He nearly said to her, "You can't run far." But she could make a clatter, and clatter she did, banging the oven door open and closed again, then swinging back one cabinet door after another as if she were searching for some particular plate she had decided would be a so much better choice than the one that was waiting on the counter. He kept on thinking Geraldine would lose her nerve and start to natter again. But it seemed that she, too, was deeply suspicious now, her body tense under his hand.

And so they waited. Robert was determined not to wade into some sprung trap. The noises Mrs Carter was making in the kitchen area gradually died away, till even she could think of nothing more she could pretend to do, and she fell silent. Lulu, still clearly lit by some strange electric charge, stepped forward till she was behind the sofa, and started dancing her pretty painted fingernails along the top of it and back, over and over.

As if he'd suddenly realized no one else was speaking, Harvey raised his eyes from the cork he was easing out of Robert's bottle, and said, "Champagne, anyone?"

There was the usual brief round of "Please!" and "A tiny bit," and "That would be very nice." As Mrs Carter took her glass she shot an anxious glance across at Lulu. Robert could not believe it was a worry about alcohol, since there was no more than a splash in Lulu's glass — barely a spoonful.

He raised his own glass. "Happy birthday, Jane!"

Out came the chorus for the second time. "Yes, happy birthday, Mum."

"And many returns."

Jane Carter still looked horribly uneasy, staring down into her glass. Then suddenly she stiffened. Here it comes, Robert thought. And, sure enough, she raised her head, slapped on her brightest face, and said in tones too shrill and brittle to be quite her own, "Well, actually, we have *two* reasons to celebrate today." She turned to Harvey. "Go on," she ordered, almost impatiently. "*Tell* them."

Robert's attention shifted from Mrs Carter's evident discomfort to Lulu. She stood there, radiating shining modesty.

"The thing is," Harvey said, "Lulu and I got married!"

200

"You got married?" Geraldine stepped forward. "A real *elopement*? Oh, how marvellous! How sweet! When did that happen?"

"Today. In Dunston."

"Today?" There was the tiniest pause as Geraldine's suspicions caught up with Robert's. Involuntarily she moved back to where she'd been before. His hand went up to keep her steady as she said in what she clearly hoped were casual tones, "I didn't think that you could do that sort of thing these days. I thought the registry offices were booked up for weeks, especially on Saturdays."

"They are," said Robert.

As Lulu smiled and Harvey beamed, Geraldine turned her eyes back on her mother. "You were there *too*?"

"Yes," said her mother with a strangled brightness. "I didn't know that it was going to happen, though. The whole thing came as a surprise to me."

Geraldine's tone had turned quite dangerous. "Really?"

"Yes." Harvey was chortling now. "The thing is that we fixed it *weeks* ago, as soon as we knew when the divorce would be through. Though I must say it was a bit of a struggle to keep the booking after we couldn't produce some stupid bit of paperwork because it hadn't yet arrived. You won't believe this, but at one point, we actually had to —"

But Geraldine wasn't even listening. She had already broken in to ask her mother, "So you had no idea at all?"

Her mother couldn't gush out excuses fast enough. "My heavens, no! Lulu had warned me to dress up a bit, but I thought that was just because of the smart place where we had lunch."

"I thought that you were going to the Frog and Spanner."

"No. That got changed." She plucked at her embroidered blouse. "So luckily, I was in this. Because, just as the three of us were passing those steps up to the Civic Hall, these two just sprung it on me."

She tried to make a little joke of it. But Geraldine didn't smile. "Told you outside? On the steps?"

"That's right. And I can't *tell* you how astonished I was. Harvey said afterwards that the look on my face was a real picture."

"You still went in, though."

There! He had been standing by, all ready to take over. But Geraldine had dared to make the point herself.

The colour flooded to her mother's face. "Well, yes, I did, dear. You see, I thought —"

"*Without* me." But she was done with her mother now. She turned to Lulu. "Why didn't you invite me?"

"Us," Robert corrected her.

"Yes, us. Why didn't you invite Robert and me to your wedding?"

Lulu reverted to the old trick of "saucer eyes" to plead her innocence. "I did invite you! Ages ago. You said you were too busy."

"Too busy to have lunch in Dunston," Geraldine replied. "We didn't say we were too busy to change things round so we could come to your wedding."

202

All Lulu did was shrug. "Oh, sorry, Geraldine. I'd no idea that you might really, really want to come."

"Mum knew, though," Geraldine turned back to face her mother. "*Didn't* you? Because I *told* you."

Jane Carter's hands were writhing in her lap. "The thing is, darling —"

But Geraldine had made her point. "Well, never mind. Too late to worry now." Putting her glass down on the coffee table, she said to Robert, "What time did you say was the latest that they let visitors in that hospital?"

Yes. Make a break for it. Smart move. Robert looked at his watch. It was a quarter to nine.

"Nine, was it?" he ventured.

"Oh, Lord!" Geraldine swept up her handbag. "All the congratulations and the details will have to wait. Jake had an accident in the lab today."

"Terrible," Robert confirmed.

"His wife's *distraught*. We promised we'd get there in time to take the baby for the night, so she can stay."

"No choice, really."

"It was our experiment."

"Bloody great flash and bang."

"Heard it four streets away."

"Even the police turned up."

"Hundreds of tiresome questions."

"Going to have a full investigation."

And they were out of the door. "Listen," called Geraldine, over the clatter of her heels down the dark stairwell, "we must have you all round for a grand celebration supper!"

"And see the photos!" Robert shouted up.

"Soon as we can!"

The huge main door swung closed behind them.

"When pigs fly!"

He let her take the wheel, as usual, but once they had driven out of sight of the flat's window, he dropped a hand on her knee. "I honestly think you ought to let me drive."

She didn't argue, just drew to a halt. He came around and opened her door for her. He even walked her to the other side. She hadn't said a thing, so he just drove off down the street with one word — "Masterly!" — and then kept quiet.

He wasn't used to having no idea at all what she was thinking. A storm was coming, surely. But of what sort? Would there be tears? Or fury? Would she vow never to speak to any of them again? Or would she force herself to understand the fix in which her mother had suddenly found herself, facing the choice of either falling in with Lulu's spiteful and divisive machinations, or plain refusing to walk up those steps into the Civic Hall?

She'd still said nothing when they reached the house. For once, she strode ahead. She didn't take her jacket off as she went through the hall. She just went straight to the kitchen. He watched from the doorway as she pulled one of the chairs away from the table and dragged it across to the cupboard. Then she climbed up to feel with her fingers for the envelope with the signed emigration application forms he'd hidden from her.

He stepped back hastily as she came past. Still rubbing smudges off the envelope, she went to the drawer and started rooting for stamps. He watched her stick on four before he cracked.

"That should be plenty!"

She still said nothing — just picked up the envelope and went to the door. He followed, staying behind her on the street. She walked as far as the corner and then turned left. He felt his heart pound. She was going to the pillar box! He turned the corner and watched from the end of the street as she took a moment to study the envelope as if to check that everything about it was fully in order — address, seal, stamps. And then she slid it into the box mouth.

He didn't utter a word when she walked back to him and slid her arm in his. Things he might say boiled in his brain, but none seemed right. And she looked so content. Her pace had slowed. Her body, leaning his way, felt perfectly relaxed. Her face was almost serene. As they walked down the street that turned into their own, he thought he saw a fat white blob squeezing its way through a hole in the hedge into a stranger's garden.

"Isn't that Puffer?"

Geraldine didn't answer, so he left her to her thoughts and they walked home in silence, arm in arm. He fished in his pocket for the key.

"Why did you even lock it?" were her first words. "We were only gone for half a tick."

"I didn't know where we were going, did I?"

This time, the moment she was through the door, she tossed her jacket over the back of a chair and looked around as if unsure of what to do. "You know, I might just have a bath and go to bed."

"Why not? A bloody long and tiring day."

"Yes, wasn't it?"

"Want me to bring you something? A bit of salad and one of your strangely sliced-up pieces of quiche?"

It worked. Reminded, she said, "Oh, my Lord! We still have to phone Martin!"

"I'll do that. He can come around tomorrow."

"Tomorrow." She said the word almost in wonder, as if it meant not just tomorrow but another life. Release. Fresh start. The works. Then she was gone. He heard the water cistern begin to roar, and when he carried up the tray a short while later, she was already steeped in bubble bath, and staring at the ceiling.

"Want to talk?"

"No."

"Later, perhaps. Well, here's your grub."

"Lovely."

He left her to it. He was free as well. No applications to take a look at one last time. No referees to phone. No point in settling down in order to refine their next experimental programme if they weren't staying.

What should he do?

Yes! He'd been putting one job off for weeks and weeks. Suddenly galvanized, Robert tugged open the drawer in which they kept most of the things he needed: scissors, a permanent marker pen, some stiff card, old-fashioned paper-reinforcing rings and a hole puncher. In Geraldine's sewing basket he found a length of scarlet ribbon from some ancient decoration. And, in her desk, a tiny square of thin, clear plastic.

That should do it nicely.

CHAPTER
TWENTY

She didn't speak about it till the following morning. "Well," she said finally across the kitchen table. "So, out with it. What do we think about all *that*?"

Robert hadn't slept. He felt like one of those political prisoners released to walk only as far as the corner ("Oh, this time! Surely *this* time!") before being arrested again. His risen hopes were almost choking him.

"Where shall we start?"

"With Mum."

She looked serene enough, but still he warned himself: go gently; don't put a single foot wrong. "You really have to take your hat off to Lulu this time," he ventured. "It was a masterly choice to put in front of someone like Jane. Pure distilled cruelty. Make a small public exhibition of the death of your toy-town image of the family, or —"

"Crap on your own daughter's head!"

He'd never heard her use that word before. He wondered if the humiliation would prove too much for her — if she would crumple. He couldn't bear that. Better to offer her some frail bridge back. "It can't have been easy for your mother."

She made a face. "What? Choosing whether to go inside and join the wedding or put her foot down?"

He nodded.

"But she knew how I *felt.*" She backtracked to be accurate. "Oh, I know none of it was strictly true, and I was covering up. But *Mum* didn't know that. She only knew that I burst into tears and told her that I'd want to be at Lulu's wedding just like everyone else. 'Popping champagne corks', I remember saying!" A thought occurred to her. "And later, when Mum caught me weeping again, she told me she *knew* exactly how happy I would be the day I watched Lulu get married. 'Generous-spirited', she called me, as I recall. 'Wonderful'. And she wasn't being sarcastic. I know that that is what she thought."

His hopes died. They were back on trampled ground. A ghastly tiredness swept over Robert. Like someone reeling out his side of a catechism, he slid into the old, old pattern. "She would, though, wouldn't she? After all, it must have been a whole lot easier for her to believe what you were saying than to face the facts."

"As ever," she agreed, and gave herself a little shake. "And as for Lulu!"

"Ah, well," he echoed. "*Lulu.*"

All this emotional havoc had not made Geraldine lose her appetite, he noticed. Now she was reaching for the last piece of toast. "It is *extraordinary*, though," she told him, slapping on marmalade.

Something about the gesture worried him. He couldn't work out what, until she pushed the jar away. The label faced him. "Geraldine —"

But she was saying it a second time. "*Extraordinary!*" And he had suddenly thought twice about the question he was planning to ask. Still utterly distracted, he only managed to gather himself enough to say, "Which bit, particularly?"

"Lulu, of course. I mean, didn't she seem happy enough to see us when we went round there to give her that present? There was no quarrel, no unpleasantness."

He thought it might be time to put her straight. "Oh, this was planned well before that."

She looked up, startled. "Really? That's what you think?"

"I'm certain. Remember that time when she was round here, claiming to be nauseous and begging for a sandwich? We couldn't understand why she had come, but she kept prowling round our kitchen."

Geraldine was appalled. "You don't think she was checking on our calendar?"

"I didn't then. But I do now."

"Trying to find out when we would be away on holiday, or have appointments, or something?"

He nodded. "I reckon, even way back then, she'd thought this caper out."

"She is *astonishing*. What is that word? *Malign*."

"Yes, she's malign."

"Small wonder that we didn't guess."

He sat in silence, wondering, What if I *had*? Relief rushed in. Thank God he hadn't picked up any of the clues — no, not the prowling round the calendar, nor the unnatural secrecy about divorce dates. Even when Geraldine reported that Lulu was apparently still spending lavishly — planning to shop for a dress and quite annoyed to think that Harvey's court date might prevent him coming with her — he hadn't given the news a second thought. Surely he should have rumbled that one! Why would someone who only had to work two days a week bother about a change of plan as trivial as that — or even want to have a man beside her as she chose?

Only, perhaps, when she had an appointment to look at bridal wear.

He had been stupid. *Stupid*. But he was so glad — so very, very glad — that he'd been blind. For he knew now that, even if he had guessed, he would have let Lulu persist in all her machinations. He would have hoped that she would go this far — yes, right up as far as this destructive and malign gesture of mischief. He would have prayed that she would get away with it. He would have even *helped* her. Anything — anything at all — that might have furnished one more tiny hope that Geraldine would say, "Enough!"

But that was obviously not going to happen. Here they were, once again, sitting together picking at the bones of one of Lulu's devilish games. Still, thanks to his own blockheadedness he could at least still look his wife in the eye. He'd not betrayed her. And so Robert sat, weak with relief that he had not been tested because he knew he would have failed, and Geraldine kept muttering, "I just don't understand it. *Why?*"

"Search me." He was just going through the motions now. They had been here a thousand times. They would be here again. As Geraldine had pointed out the day he slid the emigration form across the table and made her sign, one little sheet of paper didn't mean she had to *go*.

No. They were here for ever, locked in this family game of Psychic Tag. Dutifully he forced his attention back. "She is *unfathomable*," Geraldine was saying. "Do you suppose there's something wrong with her brain? She is a moral outsider. She doesn't even seem to *know* about the rules that others try to follow." Surprisingly, she added casually, "Do you suppose she hates me?" and then astonished him even more by answering herself. "Of course not! What a daft idea."

His disappointment made him irritable enough to shove a little penny truth across the table. "Not all *that* daft."

But she'd decided. "No, no. It's just the same old thing. Not hate. Not love. Those are about other people. This is about Lulu using everyone around her to stoke up amusement for herself. It's Lulu's hobby, and it always has been." She shrugged. "Oh, well. All I know is that I am free at last."

He stared at her. Had he heard right?

"*Free?*"

Now she was looking back at him, equally baffled. "Well, yes. Of course. I mean, why should I hang around simply to be her victim and keep providing her with all her sick excitement?"

His freshly resurrected hopes were almost choking him. He thrashed around for something — anything — to say that would not scupper things. "You're sure that's what it is?"

"Don't care." She brushed the toast crumbs off her dressing gown. "No point in trying to untangle that bitch's motives. What did you call it once? The last redoubt. Well, I'm not sure exactly what a redoubt is. But I know this is one. And it's my last." She shrugged. "And now my mother's gone and hanged herself with craven surrender . . ." She didn't even bother to end the sentence. "Are you done? Can I take your plate?"

Was *he* done? What about *her*? Was that *it*? Was it truly possible there was to be no "I am sorry if I raised your hopes." No "Look at how angry the three of them must have made me that I should have posted that stuff." No "How can we get those emigration forms back before that processing fee gets cashed?"

He had to mention them. On her response hung all his dreams of getting away, like Linda, and starting a whole new life in a fresh place.

"You could have sent the applications in on line," he said as casually as he could. "You didn't have to go along to the post."

"Perhaps. But then it wouldn't have seemed so *real*." She glanced at the clock. "What time is Martin coming?"

"Round about now."

"Whoops!" She was on her feet and off towards the stairs. And that was that. He sat there, shattered, still not sure that he had got things right. All of these years she had been working at it. All these years! She'd tried to force her mother and stepsister to be a family in the sense in which she understood the term. How was it possible that, in a single moment, she could detach

213

herself entirely from something that had used up half her life?

He thundered up the stairs behind her and beat on the shower screen. "Geraldine! Geraldine!"

"What?" Panicking, she turned off the flow of water. "What is it? What's the matter?"

"What *did* it? What made you decide?"

"For heaven's sake!" She switched the water back on and pitched her voice above it. "You know what made me decide."

"Tell me *again*. Tell me as if I were simple. Just say it. Please!"

"I can't think why you're even asking me."

"Geraldine —" His voice was on the edge of dangerous. "Tell me why you are free."

She tipped her head to rinse suds from her hair. "Because my mother truly believed that she *knew* how I felt. And she went in. *Without* me."

Simple as that. In one delicious, well-planned little act of spite, Lulu had granted him his heart's desire and set his dear wife free. Could he believe it?

Yes.

Somehow, he realized, he could.

Her mother rang in tears. "Geraldine, please!"

"No, Mum. I really haven't anything to say, and nothing you can say to me will change my views. So let's not even bother."

"I only wanted to say how very sorry I am that everything turned out that way."

"They didn't 'turn out', Mum. Lulu was vicious. And you colluded with her. No defence of your actions can hide your lack of loyalty and your lack of love for me."

"We're not on *sides*."

Geraldine let this pass.

Guilt made her mother angry. "I think you'll find grudges are ugly things, dear. They tend to rot the pocket that they're carried in."

"We could move on and talk about something else."

"It's just I wanted you to know I honestly didn't realize how upset you would be."

"Then you know very little about me. And anyway, I think you did. I think that what you're doing now is falling back on your old usual soft cushion."

"I beg your pardon?"

"Self-deception," Geraldine explained. "Pure, wilful self-deception. It runs on tracks right through your character in just the same way as cruelty runs through Lulu's."

"But Lulu is appalled as well. She didn't realize, either. She's going to ring."

"You tell her not to bother," Geraldine said. "Tell her that was the very last hoofmark that she'll be leaving on me. I will not take her calls. I do not want to see her. And if she comes round here, I'll shut the door."

"Geraldine, you don't mean this. I know you, and —"

"No," Geraldine interrupted. "You don't know me. You truly don't. You never have. What you did from the start is put your precious Lulu first because you wanted to be such a splendid stepmother." (Oh, once she was free of it, hadn't it all fallen in place!) "And then, because you felt so guilty about the effect of that on me, you found it hard to like me."

"That is the silliest thing I ever heard. It makes no sense."

"Oh, yes, it does, Mum. Because that's just how people are. They don't neglect their children because they dislike them. They dislike them because they neglect them."

"This is so overdramatic," Mrs Carter said. "You are just overwrought."

"I'm not 'just' anything," said Geraldine. "Except just finished with Lulu. And just not prepared to listen to any more excuses from you."

"Blimey," he said, dropping the phone on which he'd been eavesdropping the call back on its base. "You are in fighting trim."

"I am, aren't I?" She turned her attention immediately to the next problem. "So what are we going to do about this grisly business of offering people poisoned jobs?"

"Martin will know."

But Martin didn't. When he arrived, all that he had to offer was that he'd phoned a stockbroker he knew to check on what the rising shares might mean. As for the matter of disclosing the potential risk to the successful applicants, he had consulted with a couple of friends in other industries. And with his wife.

"Did you ask anyone in Personnel?"

"Human Resources," Geraldine corrected him.

Martin was staring at them. "Ask any of that shower? About a *moral* question?"

"No, no. Of course. You're right."

"There's only one solution, isn't there?" Geraldine announced. "We'll stall for a week or so to see if anything happens. And if it hasn't by then, I'll have to tip our chosen few the wink about the situation before I pass their names along to Dora."

"What, warn them what's going on and tell them accepting might be a gamble? You can't do that. That's a resigning matter."

"Well, that's all right, then. I'll resign." She turned to Robert. "Don't look so startled. Somebody's got to sell the cars and find a buyer for the house and choose what furniture we're taking, and all that stuff."

She was extraordinary. All of these years she'd dragged her feet and made excuses to stay. And now, like a train switched down a different track, she couldn't steam away fast enough.

Martin was mystified. "You two off somewhere?"

"Yes," Geraldine said. "We're going to Australia. We're going to live happily ever after. Just the two of us."

Robert inspected his wife's expression. It was innocent. Why was she *doing* this? Why should she choose to torment him with something that mattered so much? He couldn't help himself. In spite of the fact that Martin was on hand to listen, he just came out with it. "Geraldine, you can't keep fooling yourself much longer. It isn't going to be the *two* of us at all. There will be three."

"No," she insisted calmly. "No stepsister. No brother-in-law. Not even Mother."

So. Wrong again. She wasn't ready to admit it yet. Better to backtrack.

"You have forgotten Puffer."

But Puffer put his own future in hazard over the next few days. By Thursday Robert was spitting tintacks. "Nine people. Nine!"

"What are you on about?"

"Nine!" Robert was incensed. "After what Harvey said about seeing him on that doorstep, I thought there might be two. I even suspected that there might be three." He stared at the cat in outrage. "But nine? *Nine?*"

"Nine *what?*"

"How *dare* you!" Robert challenged Puffer. "How *dare* you, you deceitful beast!"

Geraldine rose to her feet. "If you don't tell me what is going on, I'm going to hit you."

Robert drew his attention back. He handed Geraldine a bedraggled strip of card. A shred of scarlet ribbon hung from a reinforcing ring that had come loose, and there was writing on it.

"What does it say?"

"Oh, come now. That is perfectly readable."

"Well, I can't make it out."

He rolled his eyes. "Well, what it *says*," he told her irritably, "is 'If you are feeding this cat, please let us know.' And then it gives our number."

218

"I thought there'd been a lot of calls."

"Nine! Nine bloody houses this trampy cat goes round on his perpetual trawls for grub. Small wonder he's such a *fatty!*"

"He isn't listening."

"He bloody ought to be. He is supposed to be *my* cat." Again, fury overtook him. "Not that those others know it," he snarled at Puffer. "At least four of them thought that you were *theirs*. How do you account for *that?*"

"He's still not listening."

"I'll *make* him bloody listen." And Robert bent to hiss in Puffer's ear. "This is your one and only chance. If you don't mend your ways, I'm leaving you behind. Yes, that's right! You keep this up, and I'll be cancelling your reservation in the hold. You can just stay here, and take your chances."

"They're quite good chances, actually," said Geraldine. "With all those people looking after him."

He glowered at her, then he just stormed off.

CHAPTER
TWENTY-ONE

As she was leaving the laboratory the following Tuesday, Geraldine rang her mother. She used her sunniest voice. "Oh, hi. Just checking you're around as I was thinking of popping in on my way home."

Her mother didn't even try to hide her relief. "Oh, darling! Please do!"

"Not busy? Not expecting anyone?"

"No, no."

"*Sure?*" Geraldine insisted, to make it perfectly clear that she had no desire to accidentally cross paths with Lulu.

"No, no. I'm all alone."

"Right, then. The usual twenty minutes or so."

It was a good half-hour before she reached her mother's flat. The door was open. Geraldine walked in. Her mother had already set the tray and cleared the coffee table. Jane Carter sat down warily, but gathered confidence as Geraldine discussed the steady progress of her cyclamen and sympathized sincerely with news that the lovely gabled house that formed a large part of her mother's view might be torn down to be replaced with more flats.

"Horrid! That will block quite a lot of evening sun."

"It certainly will."

On they went, talking about the various planning arguments that people whom they knew had won or lost, and the strange taste of the new brand of coffee Mrs Carter said she had picked off the shelf because she rather liked the face of the girl on the packet. Just as Jane Carter was beginning to wonder if Lulu's name would be avoided to the bitter end, her daughter popped the question.

"And Lulu? Everything going well?"

Hiding her gratitude for what she took to be the first small olive branch, Jane Carter took things gently. "She's fine, dear, though I think she's getting a little tired."

"I suppose she would by now."

"And she's moved on to some new yoga class."

"That's good."

Encouraged by Geraldine's calm tones, Jane Carter dared to embark on the sensitive task of pumping up sympathy for Lulu. "Actually, I think this whole long business might be getting her down. She said to me she thinks she is beginning to look horribly ungainly."

"Ungainly? Lulu? Never!"

Her mother smiled. "That's very sweet of you, and she'll be pleased to hear you have such confidence. But I think not fitting into any of her favourite clothes makes her feel podgy and ugly." Jane Carter linked the words "podgy" and "ugly" together as naturally as if she had been saying "peaches and cream". Geraldine forced herself not to respond, and, seeing her daughter's non-committal expression, Jane Carter suddenly felt the urge to push her even further along the path towards forgiveness. "And now, of course, the poor thing's rather stuck at home with nothing to do."

"The job's all over now, then?"

"Well, yes." Hoping that some shared confidence might prove to Geraldine that everything she'd said before about being second best was nothing short of nonsense, Jane Carter offered up the sort of snippet she would usually have kept to herself. "And I'm afraid that there are worries about Harvey's job as well."

"Really? Is his firm cutting back?"

"No, dear." Still desperate to re-entrench herself in Geraldine's good books, Jane Carter handed out the bone. "Apparently, this was a bit of nastiness at work. I'm not sure Lulu would have mentioned it, except that —"

"Except that she was touching you for a loan."

Jane Carter couldn't help reddening. "It wasn't *like* that," she began, then stopped, expecting Geraldine to pounce and tick her off for starting again down that path. But there was nothing. Geraldine was simply sitting opposite, looking quite interested and unconcerned. Startled, Jane Carter floundered on. "And it was barely anything. Just enough to pay off a couple of bills. So small I almost managed them in cash."

"Well," Geraldine said amiably, "I'm sure that you know best. What was the problem, anyway?"

"It was the electricity," said Mrs Carter. "Oh, and the council tax."

"No, no. I meant the problem with Harvey's job."

222

Her mother was far too unnerved by Geraldine's unusual complaisance to push the question away. "Oh, that. A pure misunderstanding, Harvey says. Something about a mix-up with the paperwork for a firm's car."

"Ah." Geraldine smiled again. "The car he gave Anna-Marie."

"Sorry?"

"One of his girlfriends," Geraldine explained. "It seems he bought her a car while he was having an affair with her."

Mrs Carter looked horrified. "*Affair?*"

Geraldine nodded, and reached for another of the ginger snaps. Her mother suddenly reminded her of someone in an old film. Could it be that wartime favourite, *Mrs Miniver*? She didn't know. But there was something wonderfully old-fashioned about the way she'd brought her hand up flat against her chest, as if to still a beating heart. "Affair?" Jane Carter said again. "But when was this, dear?"

Geraldine shrugged. "Not sure. Quite recently, I understand, because the car in question was only one or two years old."

"How do you *know* all this?"

"From Linda," Geraldine explained through crumbs. "You know. His former wife. She mentioned it to Robert."

The shock was obvious. "I didn't know that you two knew Harvey's wife!"

"We don't," said Geraldine. "Not really. It's just that whenever she and Robert happen to meet when they're out shopping, they tend to have a little chat." She reached down for her bag. "Oh, well," she told her mother cheerfully. "Speaking of Robert, I told him I would only be half an hour or so, and we have plans tonight. So I had better be off."

She left her mother too punch drunk even to see her to the door.

She offered up the warning even as she walked through the door. "Lulu-watch! She is on the cadge."

"Too late," said Robert. "Harvey already rang."

"Harvey? You're joking!"

"Scout's honour. As I live and breathe. The telephone was ringing as I came through the door. I missed it, but it rang again within ten minutes."

Geraldine flung herself on the sofa. "Tell all. No! Let's make a pleasure of it. Make me a gin and tonic first."

She sat there wriggling her toes as he went off. When he came back, it was with wine. "Sorry, clean out of gin."

"Really?" But it was clear she didn't really care. She sipped the wine. "Go on! How, in the circumstances, did the man have the bare-arsed cheek to even *start* to go about the business of touching us for a loan?" She took another sip. "This wine tastes very odd."

"I thought that, too," he said. "Acceptable, though."

But she had risen to her feet and gone to fetch the bottle. She came back brandishing the label. "Non-alcoholic!" she read out. "Organic grapes. Silicates-free."

Again, he waited. Was this, then, the time to speak up? But it was not. Already she was settling back on to the sofa. "Oh, well. Get on and tell the story."

Shaking his head in wonder, both at his wife and the sheer nerve of her new brother-in-law, Robert took up the tale. "He started off with a few pleasantries. The shocking weather. Who won last night's match. That sort of thing. And then he got into gear. He did admit the two of them might have been a little tactless —"

"Tactless!"

"But he said there was something that I really had to know because, whatever the current niggles —"

"Niggles!"

"— between two rather excitable women might be —"

"Ah, ha! Unfaithful, grasping *and* sexist!"

"— there was something *important*. And then he pressed on, taking the 'pregnant woman's health' line. He almost made her sound as if she were some starving child in the third world. He said that for various reasons things were a little tight at present for the two of them, and all they needed was a little loan to tide them over. The sort of loan, he said, that probably wouldn't mean a thing to us because we had such steady jobs and such good incomes, and yet to them could mean the difference between poor Lulu eating the right sort of food through a critical part of her pregnancy or eating worms."

"Harvey did not say worms!"

"Well, no. But almost."

Geraldine reached forward to top up her glass.

"Hey," Robert warned. "Go easy. There's organic water in that. Without any silicates. So you watch out."

She smiled. "So what did you say?"

"Well, I began by stalling, naturally. I think I said that I was certainly a little surprised to hear from him on any matter at all, given the way things had been. He couldn't jump in fast enough. It was quite clear he'd been rehearsed on his lines. He said he thought that he and Lulu had been very remiss in not making absolutely sure that we had understood it was the *wedding* they were talking about when they invited us that Saturday."

"Oh, she is glorious!"

"But he knew I would understand that Lulu is in a very delicate state, and it's not good for her or the baby to have so many worries."

"Ah, yes," said Geraldine. "The electricity bill. The council tax."

"How did you know?"

"Mum. She paid up."

"Well, that's all right, then," Robert said cheerfully. "Because I'm afraid I simply didn't know what to do at that point. So I just took the coward's line — suddenly started repeating, 'Sorry, Harvey? Are you still there? Can you hear me?' over and over for half a minute or so, then pulled the phone plug out." He waved a hand behind her. "And it's still out."

"He's lost his job, you know," said Geraldine.

And as her husband reached for the glass of orange he had privately laced with the gin he'd hidden in the guest room along with all the proper wine, she trumped his rather wonderful new story with hers.

There was a letter in Geraldine's pigeon-hole the following morning. Before she had even managed to unfold it properly, Martin was leaning across to read it over her shoulder. "So? What have you got?"

"Sorry?"

He ran his finger down her letter. "See? There. Eighteen. That's nowhere near as good as me, but then again, I've been here that much longer."

She tried to concentrate. "What is it on about?"

"Redundancy!" he told her. "Didn't you realize? Thirty-five thousand, I'm getting, just to pack my bags. It's not bad, eh?"

She stared at the host of drab grey envelopes sticking out of the pigeon-holes. "Have we *all* got one?"

"No, no," said Martin. He waved a hand towards a couple of empty boxes on the shelves. "They're clearly keeping Geoffrey's lab. And Anita and her gang are safe. I rather think they'll get the call to move to Croydon very soon, though. No one will want to keep this giant tub of a building going once they've got rid of all of us."

All of us. And it did look as if there were a lot of them who'd had the final flick. The corridor was buzzing, and a meeting had been called for ten. All the way along to the cafeteria, Geraldine tried her hardest to keep her face grave, but she was singing inside. Rounding the corner she bumped into Dora, who was

227

scurrying back to her office after a quick trip to the Ladies'.

"My new appointments," Geraldine tackled her. "Those names we're planning to give you. What will happen to them?"

Dora shook her head. "God, Geraldine. I am so sorry. I had heard *hints*, of course, but . . ."

So. One more worry off her mind. Not even stopping to berate poor Dora for wasting three weeks of her life with all the applications and the interviews, she sailed on by. What were three tiresome weeks against a whole new life? Fair trade indeed! She'd make sure Dora rang all nine, in case they were still standing by. But that would be the end of things. The very end.

Job over.

Robert's as well. And he was cock-a-hoop. "Hey! Sixteen thousand! You do realize what this could mean? It is enough for a down payment on another house."

"Another?"

"In Melbourne. When the paperwork comes through. We could leave ours in the hands of an agent till it sells, and just take off." He didn't stop to talk about it any more. Already he was off along the corridor, waving his letter and trying to catch up with Jake, who'd just gone round the corner.

Geraldine wandered into her laboratory. Did she mind breaking off and leaving her research? No, she decided. Once the whole head is off, why should one grieve about the hair? She would still have her brain, her knowledge and experience. There would be great excitement in starting over. It wasn't as if she had been toiling for the last eight years for one particular result, only to have it snatched away at the last minute. So she would just be grateful that leaving Delwort and Price had been so easy.

CHAPTER
TWENTY-TWO

Robert caught her leaning over the lavatory, holding her hair back from her face. "Hey!"

She turned, eyes shining from the effort of blinking back tears. He turned on the tap and waited till the water ran hot. He held a flannel under the flow, then squeezed it out and handed it to her. When she had finished mopping her face, he passed a towel. "Better?"

She nodded.

He took her hand and led her back into the bedroom. Pushing her down gently on to the edge of the bed, he said, "Sit there. Don't move."

Down in the kitchen he pulled the wooden spoon out of the jar on the counter, then ran back upstairs. Behind her back, he tugged the little stripy hat out from where she had hidden it all those weeks before. Pulling it over the spoon's head at a rakish angle, he came to sit beside her on the bed. "We can't go on like this. We have to have a little talk."

She stared at the hat on the spoon.

"We three," he prompted. "We're a family now."

She still looked blank. "Geraldine," he said. "Please tell me that you're faking this. Please tell me that I haven't married someone so thick and stubborn that even while she's throwing up into the lavatory bowl she can't accept she's pregnant."

He watched her face. He'd only seen that look of pure shock once before, and that was when, crossing a road, she'd missed death by an instant.

"Pregnant?"

He spread his hands. "Geraldine, you've been eating like a horse for three whole weeks. You have developed a passion for ginger biscuits, ginger cake and ginger marmalade. Ginger marmalade, Geraldine! You've always hated ginger marmalade. Hated it! And you are throwing up. There is no little circle on the calendar." He waggled the stripy hat on the spoon. "What me and the baby want to know is, what do *you* think is happening?"

"The baby?" A look of wonder crossed her face as she stretched out her hand and touched the little stripy hat. "Truly?"

"*I* think so. So does the hat. And wouldn't you, if you were not too scared to even start to think we might be lucky at last?"

"Oh, God! A baby!"

"You just sit there," he said. He folded her hand around the wooden spoon handle and anchored it more safely on the bed. "You hold the baby and I'll go and get the stick you pee on, and some ginger tea."

"You've actually bought a tester?"

Robert shook his head at her. "For heaven's sake! I have been sitting waiting for ten whole days, hiding the gin, decanting organic cat's pee into proper wine bottles and grinding folic acid pills on to your food. Of *course* I've bought a tester. Just because *you've* temporarily gone a little daffy . . ."

She didn't hear the rest. He'd disappeared into the closet, where he was rooting through his jacket pockets for the small packet from the pharmacist. She sat and stared at the spoon. A baby, then. At last. It still did not seem possible.

When he came out, the wooden spoon was lying abandoned on the bed. The hat had fallen off, and she was back beside the lavatory. Down his wife's shining face tears rolled unchecked, only to tremble on her chin and nose, and plop into the water.

"What did you *think*?" he asked an hour or so later, when she was feeling better. "How on earth did you explain the morning throw-ups to yourself?"

She started weeping again.

"See?" he crowed. "Emotionally labile. That's another sign."

"Actually," she said, already laughing through her tears, "I thought that I was scared of telling Mum that we were leaving."

"Really?" He frowned. "I think you'd probably better get that over with, then, in case it really starts to worry you."

"Maybe I should."

"Do you want moral support?"

"I'll have a think about that."

"Well," he warned, "while you are busy pondering on that one, perhaps we should also work out what to do when Harvey rings again."

"You're sure he will?"

"He has already. Several times."

"Really? I didn't know."

"That is because I've been deleting messages and doctoring phones. But it's been four days now. We can't keep on pretending that all of our means of communication are on the blink."

"I suppose we can't."

She munched her toast. Assuming that, unusually, his wife had no plan in mind, he said, "I thought we might just slip them a few hundred pounds and hope it keeps them going until we've scarpered."

"Why would we do that? They would just be back again, asking for more."

"It'll be easier to ignore them from all that way away."

"Why?"

For the life of him he wasn't sure. "I just thought that it would be."

"It won't, though. A begging phone call is a begging phone call, wherever in the world you are."

"I suppose it is. Got any better ideas?"

"Well, yes," she said. "Plan A. I am not giving them a single penny. They blew their chances of my acting like a family member two weeks ago. I am not mean. If you tell me how much you think we would have given them, I'll choose a charity of my choice. But it will not be them."

He stared. "You mean it, don't you?"

She wasn't even looking tense. She wasn't looking angry or harsh. She just looked like someone who'd thought things through and had decided on the better path. "Yes. Yes, I do. I'll prove it, too. How much do you think we'd have given them? Tell me. Go on. I bet, given the chunks of money we just found out we're getting, it would have been a lot. Well, right now I am going to write a cheque. And it'll be for those who've had a bloody sight fewer chances in life than either of those two." For the first time, she scowled. "And very probably behaved much better."

"Good for you!" he responded automatically, then sat back watching her across the table and wondering if that was truly what he thought. Were they at one on this? Or was some part of him appalled that she was suddenly so firm and tough?

Not that he knew. No. He could stand four-square with her on this, as on so many other things. What she was planning to do was no more than he had been urging her to do all down the years. It was exactly what his own parents had said so often all those years ago: "Everyone should stop indulging Lulu. All of this spoiling simply makes her worse."

He took another tack. "The baby, though?"

But Geraldine had clearly thought that through as well. "She'll manage. I'm sure between the two of them they'll winkle quite enough out of my mother to keep the wolf from the door."

"You're sure, then?" He left the table and went to the phone. Here was the test. "You're sure enough for me to put the batteries back in this thing?"

"And all the others. And you can switch your mobile on as well."

234

He made a face. "No fear! Not till *you*'ve spoken to them both."

She grinned. "You needn't worry. I'm not going to *quarrel* with them."

"Brag when it's over," he warned. And then he wailed. "Oh, God! I bet they ring while I am at the shops, and I'll miss all the joy of hearing it."

But her attention was lost. "Are you off to the shops? Well, can you get noodles with scallops and ginger? And some more ginger marmalade. And —"

"Hang on," he said. "Don't get your hopes up. You won't believe the number of things I've been avoiding buying. Just let me check." He pulled out the list he'd downloaded from the internet and ran his eyes down all the rules on pregnant women and fish. "Let's see, now. Scallops . . ." He raised his head. "Yes, we're all right, so long as they are thoroughly cooked. 'Opaque and firm.'" He sighed. "Actually, *ruined* seems to be more the word."

Geraldine didn't care. She was already going off to look up morning sickness and its various cures. And when she wandered back to crow at him that ginger marmalade was just the thing, he had already gone.

The phone rang while he was still out of the house. Geraldine stared at it. She had been honest when she said she wasn't scared to pick it up, but she just let it ring until the answer phone kicked in. Robert had clearly programmed the machine to record silently while he was dealing with the messages he had been hiding. So she just waited till the little light went out, then pressed the button.

The voice was Lulu's, sounding perfectly firm and confident. "Oh, hi! It's me again. Look —"

With no more interest or emotion than she'd have used to cut off some bright electronic voice imploring her to think about her need for double glazing, Geraldine pressed down her finger and the voice cut off.

"Sorry," she told her stepsister. "I have deleted you. Try again later."

Then she went off to make a list of all the things she'd need to bring home from the laboratory over the next few weeks.

That evening, after giving it a great deal of thought, she went to see her mother on her own. Robert hovered over her as she got in the car. "Sure you don't want me with you?"

"Absolutely sure."

He nearly asked her, "Will you be telling your mother about the baby?" but bit the words back in the nick of time. If he knew anything at all about his wife, it was that she would very sensibly keep her own counsel about that till a few more weeks had passed and she could be a bit more confident about their luck.

"Well, you go easy."

But she spun along at the same speed as usual. Only when she was pulling in beside the flats did she remember what she'd come to talk about. All of her thoughts on the short drive had been about the lab.

236

Each time the fact that she was pregnant came to mind, she'd forced the thought away. Not yet. Too precious. So, not yet.

A watery half-smile was all her mother offered as she opened the door. "Come in, dear."

Geraldine slid off her jacket. "You look a little tired, Mum."

Her mother seemed a bit put out at the sheer speed at which her daughter had appeared to take the hint. Perhaps, thought Geraldine, she would have liked to play the Martyr Queen a little longer. Still, she rallied fast. There was a touch of sharpness in her tone as she responded. "Are you surprised? I can have had barely a *wink* of sleep since your last visit."

"What, worrying about Lulu?"

"Of course! What did you think? That you could simply tell me all those tales about Harvey, and I'd be able to put it straight out of my mind?"

Ah, ha! So "tales" was what the information had become. Nothing to do with Harvey's behaviour. Jane clearly preferred to make things sound as if her daughter had been acting like a child, sneaking unnecessarily. Geraldine turned away to hide her smile. Oh, if her mother was going into battle, then this whole business was going to be a whole lot easier than she had thought. Prudently draping her jacket over the chair nearest the door, she chose her most repentant tone to say, "I'm sorry. I had no idea that you would rather not have known."

Her mother gave her a cold look, then moved away towards the kitchen. "I'm not saying that. All that I'm saying is — Oh, bother!" And she took the opportunity

237

of a quick spill of coffee grounds across the counter to busy herself with a damp cloth and change the subject. "Anyhow, what is this Robert mentioned on the phone about your jobs?"

Geraldine froze. This came as a surprise. She knew that Robert was in seventh heaven. Only this morning she'd heard him chatting to a quite baffled Latvian in the corner shop about the weather in Perth. Still, she'd not realized he had told her mother.

She stalled. "I won't have coffee." Then, fearing to leave a single speck of evidence about her pregnancy behind her, she added hastily, "That stupid car heater is on the blink again. I almost fried on the way over, and my throat's parched. Can I have juice?" She stepped around her mother to open the fridge. "I didn't know that Robert told you we were being made redundant."

"Redundant?" Her mother turned to stare. "He didn't tell me that!"

So. One more hurdle sailed over without much effort simply because of a misunderstanding. Things were going well. "What *did* he say?"

"Just that the firm was looking a lot more unsettled this week than last."

"Not half!" said Geraldine. "We think that most of it is closing down. And all the rump is getting moved to Croydon."

"*Croydon?*" Her mother gave the most genteel of northern shudders. "I'm not surprised you'd rather take redundancy."

"Actually, Robert and I have no choice."

"No choice?"

238

Geraldine picked up the tray and carried it through to the sitting room. "Not really, no. We'll all be leaving in a matter of weeks. I have to close down the lab. All that recruiting we've been doing recently has been a waste of time. And Robert and I were sent our marching orders, just like everyone else."

It was as if the news had drained her mother of hostility. "Oh, this is terrible." She shook her head. *"Terrible!"* She sounded perfectly sincere, and Geraldine warmed to her, especially when she added, after a moment, "Though, frankly, dear, I do believe that you and Robert will have very little trouble finding new jobs. Do you have anything in mind?"

"Well, yes, we do," admitted Geraldine. Here came the biggest hurdle. Was she up to it? Taking the deepest breath, she launched off. "But that involves a bigger change all round."

Her mother raised her coffee cup and waited for the blow she was expecting. "Oh dear. I suppose you're worrying it might entail a move?"

"That's right. In fact, we're going the whole hog. We're going to pack up the house and move to Melbourne."

Her mother's coffee cup had frozen in mid air.

"And we'll not bother," Geraldine pressed on, "to look for jobs until we get there. Both of us think that would be far more sensible. And —"

"Geraldine!" It was the sort of tone you took with a dog you had caught scratching a rug. "Geraldine, I'm not sure that I'm following!"

Geraldine said it again. "Robert and I are going to Australia."

It was as if her mother was offering her one last chance to back down quietly. "But for how *long*, dear?"

"Actually, for good." Geraldine forced herself not to start gabbling out of sheer nervousness. "Unless we hate it, of course, in which case we'll come back. Or move on somewhere else."

"You're actually *emigrating*?"

"We thought so, yes."

Her mother was appalled, that much was evident. That look of shock and horror could not be feigned. But then there came another little miracle to rescue Geraldine in her plight. The words just popped out of Jane Carter's mouth. "But, darling, what about *me*?"

Could she have made it easier? No. This clear, uncluttered glimpse of how she viewed the world around her was enough to see her daughter through. Reaching for yet another of the ginger biscuits, Geraldine said amiably, "Well, you could *come*, of course. Sell this place. Buy a flat in Melbourne. I'm not quite certain of the rules, but I am sure they must include *some* way of bringing out people's relations."

Her mother's face took on the look of a burnt slipper. "And suppose, at my age, I don't feel inclined to start uprooting myself and moving halfway across the world?"

But it was done now. Finally seeping into Geraldine's consciousness was the awareness that she'd actually done it. She'd told her mother! The sheer relief of having the task behind her turned her mischievous. "You're not too old," she scolded cheerfully in an encouraging fashion. "Look at you. You're fit as a flea. Your brain's in perfect working trim. You know that

Robert's parents would be neighbourly and introduce you to all their friends. And you could join a bridge club."

Her mother took revenge. As Geraldine reached forward, she asked, "Are you quite sure you want another biscuit, darling? That is your fourth."

Oh, so, *so* easy now. "You're right! I'm not going to look that brilliant on Bondi beach, am I, if I'm as fat as a pig?"

"I think you'll find that Bondi beach is actually in Sydney."

Unruffled by the correction, Geraldine responded, "Oh, well. I expect we'll travel. After all, we'll want to see around. And so must you! If you don't want to emigrate along with us, you must come out as often as you like, and stay for ages."

Her mother's voice took on a tone intended to make her daughter understand that, though she herself might think of her own pleasure, others had duty in their path. "Aren't you forgetting someone?"

"Am I?" asked Geraldine innocently. "Who is that?"

"Lulu. I think we were agreed that she was going to need all the support that she can get."

"She rather blew that, didn't she," Geraldine said cheerfully, "by engineering things the way she did about the wedding."

Jane Carter laced her next response with some disdain. "You're surely not still holding *that* against her! Not with this baby on his way."

"Another son, then?" Geraldine slid in spitefully. "I hope that Harvey isn't too awfully disappointed at missing out on having a daughter third time around."

She added almost as an afterthought, "Or, of course, if Linda has a boy as well, fourth time."

"That is unworthy of you," Mrs Carter said.

Geraldine lost her temper. "It probably is. I think the problem is that I am sick to death of being the only one who always tries to behave well!"

A look of sheer contempt came over her mother's face. "You're *still* not over that? You're *still* accusing me of acting badly towards you?"

Oh, why not say it? "Yes, I am. I think you shouldn't have gone into that wedding ceremony. That's what I told you afterwards. And I *still* think it."

Her mother wasn't used to seeing her so angry. She started sounding more conciliatory. "But, Geraldine, I did try hard to make things clear to you." She spread her hands. "They sprung it on me. It was a surprise. And obviously I didn't want to make a fuss — not on their wedding day!"

Geraldine made a massive effort to step around that raw spot. "We won't go over that again. No point. But you must understand that I myself have had enough of thinking about Lulu — especially when every thought that Lulu has ever had about me seems to have been either to do with making me feel fat and boring, or about how to winkle money out of me."

"Oh, really, Geraldine!"

But Geraldine wouldn't stop. "So from now on, she and her sleazy husband can go ahead and run their lives without my help."

Her mother murmured, "Geraldine, if you could only *hear* yourself . . ."

242

"You think I'd be disgusted? I'm not so sure. Perhaps, on the contrary, I'd think I'd finally grown up and faced the truth of my relationships."

Her mother's voice packed thirty years of gathered scorn. "Scarcely grown up, to run away across the world simply because you've been upset by your sister!"

"*Stepsister*, thank you. And after the divorce, she wasn't even that." Geraldine shook her head. "No, Mum. You made a choice on Lulu's wedding day. And you can make a choice again, any time you choose. You will be welcome to come out with us. Or, if you want to visit for a while, to see the place and nose around a bit to see if it'll suit you, that'll be fine with us too."

Her mother panicked. "You're not really going, dear?" In desperation, she took another tack. "Frankly, I am surprised at Robert."

"Robert?"

"Yes. Letting you make such an enormous decision while you are still so upset about Lulu making that horrible mistake about your invitation."

Oh, ho! So she had swallowed Harvey's line. And why not? It made a better whitewash for her own sins. But Geraldine had had enough of arguing with her mother. She'd promised Robert that they wouldn't quarrel, and here they were, already at loggerheads. Rather than press on and say anything more, she would ignore that red rag. "You've got it wrong," she tried to correct her mother. "It isn't me who wanted to run away because I was 'upset'. Robert has wanted to do this for nearly ten years."

Her mother's lip deliberately curled. "Oh, Robert!"

And Geraldine was suddenly fifteen years old again, flushing beet red as Lulu and her mother exchanged their usual glance across the table. "Oh, Robert!" one or the other would be saying, her mother with a soft, forgiving smile, and Lulu with a smirk. Who found your pencil box? Oh, Robert! Who's taking you to the dance? Oh, Robert! Who gave you that pretty ring? Oh, Robert. Only Robert. As if he didn't count. As if he were just some pitiful skivvy from next door and his attentions were so cheap they counted for no more than beans.

Geraldine took a good look at her mother. She felt as if a glass wall had dropped down between the two of them. She felt quite calm. What did it matter what her mother thought? She'd lost all moral credibility. All Geraldine wanted now was to get out of there without another fight.

"Well, there you go." She shrugged. "He just came home the day after the wedding, and told me we had waited long enough, and he had filled in the forms."

"What? *Sprang* it on you? Just like that? But that's outrageous, darling!"

Geraldine shrugged. "Oh, I don't know. Surely it's much the same as Lulu springing the wedding on you."

Surely her mother saw the trap open in front of her? Apparently not. "But you can tell him you don't want to go!"

"I suppose I didn't want to disappoint him." Yes! That was the line to take. Little Miss Perfect. "*Or* cause unpleasantness. And he's so very *happy* with the idea. I really wouldn't want to spoil that." Hoping that her expression was quite as bland as those on the faces of

244

the china dolls that irritated Lulu, she shrugged again. "So I suppose I did exactly the same as you did at the wedding — just went along with it."

Clearly her mother burned with exasperation. "But, Geraldine, the two things aren't in the slightest comparable. This is *important!*"

"Oh, I don't know. Once you begin to dig, don't you find out that what's important to one is often not at all the same as what matters to another? You keep on telling me you think I'm being foolish to make a fuss about the wedding. 'It's not a battle, Geraldine,' you keep on saying. 'We're not on *sides*.' And I think you'll find that, what with these easy ways to keep in touch that we have now, this'll turn out to be much the same. Not at all important."

Geraldine reached for her bag. Inside, the whole of her was praying her mother wouldn't reel her back. Don't weep, she begged her silently. Don't sag. Don't sit there, please, looking as if the stuffing's falling out of you. I couldn't bear it. I would only crack.

But there was nothing, just a steady look as the silence between them lengthened. It lasted far too long. Eventually Geraldine picked up her coat, murmured goodbye and shut the door gently behind her. And when she told Robert about the visit, half an hour later, she still didn't know whether to add the words she thought her mother might have called after her along the carpeted passage.

"Geraldine, you are a *bitch*. A goody-goody *bitch!*"

Or whether she had simply forged the echo of them out of her own guilt.

CHAPTER
TWENTY-THREE

"Yoga? But you've not been for weeks and weeks."

"I'll take it gently." She caught his anxious look. "Look, Robert, I'm not *Puffer*. I can't sit in a cosy chair for eight whole months. For heaven's sake, why not?"

And for the life of him he couldn't think of any sensible reason. She did look fit enough, standing there in her track pants and wearing that flowery short-sleeved top they'd bought in Athens. "I suppose it can't hurt. But are you sure that Lulu won't be there?"

"I checked. The class for anyone as pregnant as she is now is on a Tuesday." (How strange, she thought, to hear herself say the word "pregnant" without that old familiar pang.) She reached behind the sideboard to slide out the mat. "Expect me back around eight."

He watched from the window as she got in the car and backed it on to the street. Got to stop worrying, he told himself. Women get pregnant all the time. Nothing will happen.

But something did. Five minutes into the class, the swing doors creaked. Geraldine glanced across, and it was Lulu. Thank God she hadn't moved her head. At least she could pretend she hadn't noticed till she'd decided what to do.

The instructress padded over towards the doors. Even before Lulu could spread her mat, she'd been taken aside. Was it to be offered a warning? But Lulu clearly gave some sort of answer that would satisfy. Perhaps she had promised not to attempt the more testing poses. So, throughout the class, with all its gentle urgings to "Stretch that out as long as possible," there came the added murmurs, "Lulu, keep your feet tucked in for this one, please," and "Not you, Lulu. You just stay the way you are through this next bit."

And on they'd go. But it was nothing but a wasted hour for Geraldine. Clumsily she distorted herself into one tiresome pose after another, her only thoughts on that black-clad body by the door who would be watching. Had Lulu come only in the hope of catching her? Whenever Geraldine had to turn her head towards the doors, she closed her eyes, as though in concentration. Now there were only twenty minutes to go — unless she simply grabbed her mat and made a run for it.

What was the point? Lulu would only follow. Ten minutes left. Just ten short minutes in which to make up her mind whether, when Lulu finally came over with that triumphant "Got you!" grin, it would be best to slap her, cut her dead, or lend her money.

The class drew to an end. And with the usual gentle wrap-up line of "Thank you, ladies. Nice class," the women who had families waiting promptly picked up their mats and crept away, leaving the others lying in their last relaxed position.

No point in putting this off. Geraldine scrambled to her feet. "Hi, Lulu. Come to find me?"

"Of course not. I just felt a little stiff and thought I'd come and do the easy bits."

"How is it going?" asked Geraldine. And even as the words popped out, she wondered why she felt obliged to keep the conversation going. If Lulu wanted money, then let her set about working to get it. So Geraldine waited as the bulletins tripped out: "Feeling quite marvellous, really . . . can fit in hardly any clothes . . . appointment at the clinic."

They'd reached the street where Geraldine had parked. She spoke at last. "I'm off down here."

Lulu stepped out in front of her. "Don't hurry away. Can't we go off and have a drink together? This has been so upsetting, this horrible misunderstanding about the wedding."

She felt like saying, "Frankly, Lu, I would as soon be locked all night in a fridge as have a chat with you." But in the end she settled for a casual, "No, I don't think so."

"You're not still in a *stew*?" A knowing smile spread over Lulu's face. "Or is this Robert, finally managing to push you into blocking me out of your life?"

And once again, the path was clear. How could these cunning and manipulative people make such a big mistake? Did they assume that everybody's clockwork ticked in the same way as theirs? The trouble with Lulu had always been that she didn't know who her friends were. Did she not realize that others did? She might, like Jane, assume that Geraldine could be quite easily riled into a quick reversal of her plans by the suggestion that she, who'd thought herself an equal partner all her life, in the laboratory and in the home, was simply bowing to a man's desires. Could neither of them guess that someone like Geraldine might recognize who was her rock and her support — the man who would eke out his whole life where he no longer wanted to be, simply because he loved her.

Robert.

She wouldn't fall into the old trap of arguing. There Lulu stood, waiting for her to snap, "This isn't anything to do with Robert," or "I'm not in a stew." She felt her silence as chain mail that was protecting her as she walked off. And she kept walking as Lulu hurried beside her. "God, aren't you even *speaking* to me now? Look, come for a drink. I want to tell you something."

But Geraldine had reached her car. She turned. "Lulu, whatever it is, I don't want to hear it. And I don't want to listen to excuses, or be touched for a loan. I don't want to hear you talk about me, or my life or my husband. I don't want you to tell me anything. All of my life, when I've spent time with you, I've felt far, far worse afterwards than I did before. And I don't want that any more, so I am going home. You do the same. Then you can live your life and I'll live mine."

There. Easy!

Geraldine swung the car door open and clambered in. By the time she had turned the key to start the engine, Lulu was hopping anxiously from one foot to the other. "Geraldine, you're just not thinking."

Geraldine started backing towards the bumper of the car behind. She turned the wheel. Could it be done in one? Probably not.

"This is ridiculous!" called Lulu through the glass. "You can't just decide that you're not going to have anything to do with me."

Geraldine let down the window. "Oh, yes, I can." Tugging the wheel, she moved the car carefully back and forth, easing the wheels round.

Lulu tried playing one more card. "But what about your mother?"

Now Geraldine was finally at an angle where she could safely drive away. "Mum?" she called as she pulled out into the empty street. "No problem, Lulu. I've a really good idea that solves that problem. You and Harvey have her."

All the way to the corner her brain was echoing with some old phrase that had run through her brain so many months ago.

Winner takes all.

"You *gave* her Jane?"

"More or less, yes. I mean, the two of them are bound to end up bleeding her dry in any event. So I just thought I'd offer them my blessing."

"Cor blimey, Geraldine! And then you just drove off?"

"That's right."

He turned to Puffer. "What do you think of that?" He turned back. "Sweetie pie, I have to ask you one more serious question. Do you feel guilty?"

Did she? She'd given it some thought, both times — after she was so firm with Jane and when she left Lulu. She'd tried to look into her soul and answer honestly. She did the same again. "No," she said. "No, I don't. I did with Mum, for just a minute, till I got out of the building and safely back in the car. But I think that was nothing more than habit. It soon wore off. And I had warned her, after all. I'd made it perfectly clear that I thought she had let me down by never once taking a stand on my behalf. So now, as far as I can tell, everyone in this family has got exactly what they ordered. Why should I feel any guilt?"

He left it there, of course. Whistling some tune about setting sail and facing rolling billows, he went off to heat up the soup he'd made for her return. She knew that he would ask again. And maybe, soon, the answer would be different. But she imagined that there'd never be a moment when she could tell him, "This is what I feel," and have it stand as truth for evermore. Part of the time she probably would feel guilty. The rest she probably wouldn't (leaving aside the many times when she might not be quite sure). But surely the worst crime of any war was to have started it. And she had not done that. No. She had even put off opening hostilities until she had no choice. To save herself, she'd had to stand and fight.

And she had won.

So she felt pity, but no remorse. They would both cope. Maybe, for Lulu, leeching off Jane would not provide anything like as much amusement as tormenting Geraldine had done over the years. But she had not been put upon this planet to offer entertainment to her stepsister. She'd done it long enough. Time to move on.

And that is what it felt like. For truly it did seem as if things in her world had fallen out so she could walk out of the bog of cruelty that had formed round her through the years. Now she could treat her future as if it were a blank room she could fill from scratch — not just the sticks of furniture, but everything — *everything* — down to the wallpaper and door knobs. A whole new place where she was going to live.

Free. And away.

The weeks would roll along. One day, the paperwork would come, paving the way. They'd book the flights. The house would soon be cleared. Maybe there would be tenants, maybe not. But one day, not too far along the line, the sales papers would be exchanged and that part of their life would finally be over.

With or without Puffer, they would get on the plane. "I'm going to let you have one little swig from my celebration gin and tonic," he would offer her. But she would run her arms protectively around her belly and shake her head. She wouldn't need the tiniest sip of alcohol to celebrate this flight. The quiet and bone-soothing sound of throbbing engines carrying them away for ever would be quite enough.

Also available in ISIS Large Print:

Breathing in Colour

Clare Jay

"Your child is missing — presumed dead."

Hours after receiving the phone call that every mother dreads, Alida Salter flies to India to search for her backpacker daughter.

Mia is no ordinary girl. Growing up with the sensory condition synaesthesia — where she sees the world in a kaleidoscope of shapes, colours and smells — she has gone through life with the vivid imagination of an artist, but for years she has shouldered an overwhelming burden of guilt. It has been a difficult relationship, but now comes the toughest test of all . . . How far will a mother go to find her missing daughter?

ISBN 978-0-7531-8496-7 (hb)
ISBN 978-0-7531-8497-4 (pb)

December

Elizabeth H. Winthrop

A descriptive tour de force   **New York Times**

It's December in New England, season of snow, log fires and happy family Christmases. Except not for the Carters. Eleven-year-old Isabelle hasn't spoken for months, countless experts have given up on her, and her parents are at their wits' end. Gnawing away at them is the thought that it must be their fault, and that their daughter's life might be ruined for good. Something has to give . . .

In this superbly wrought novel, taut with tension, Elizabeth Winthrop portrays a marriage beginning to crack under pressure and a girl whose attempt to control her universe locks her into self-imposed silence.

ISBN 978-0-7531-8462-2 (hb)
ISBN 978-0-7531-8463-9 (pb)

Fly in the Ointment

Anne Fine

Guilt is in the eye of the beholder

"Guilt's in the eye of the beholder. So you tell me what you think you'd have done. You be the judge."

When, like her cold and indifferent husband, Lois's old life vanishes into thin air, she can't help snatching at the opportunity to come alive.

There's only one fly in the ointment: Janie Gay, the feckless and spiteful mother of her wayward son's child. But as Lois takes her second — and redeeming — chance at love, she finds herself on a collision course with a society that claims to support and protect. Suddenly it seems that all those years of nurturing her own deep-frozen heart may not have been so wasted after all . . .

ISBN 978-0-7531-8102-7 (hb)
ISBN 978-0-7531-8103-4 (pb)

Consequences

Penelope Lively

A hugely satisfying and romantic novel

Three generations of 20th-century women: a young woman, her daughter and her granddaughter, their contrasting lives and their achievement of love.

Lorna escapes her conventional Kensington family to marry artist Matt, but the Second World War puts an end to their immense happiness. Molly, their daughter, will have to wait longer to find love and Ruth, Lorna's granddaughter, even longer still: an enthralling examination of interweaving love and history.

ISBN 978-0-7531-7992-5 (hb)
ISBN 978-0-7531-7993-2 (pb)

Raking the Ashes

Anne Fine

Lovers, colleagues, family — Tilly has always been brilliant at pushing people in and out of her life exactly as it suits her. Then along comes Geoffrey, gentle, compassionate, generous to a fault, with his miserable little children and his manipulative ex-wife.

Tilly's own expertise in the arts of deception and avoidance should be enough to make sure she's always one step ahead of Geoffrey's wretched crumbling family. But time and again she finds herself staying, brought down by their cowardly backsliding and their barefaced lies.

How has she managed to stay so long in a relationship that she knows perfectly well has to be doomed? More importantly, how can Tilly plan her permanent escape?

ISBN 978-0-7531-7403-6 (hb)
ISBN 978-0-7531-7404-3 (pb)

ISIS publish a wide range of books in large print, from fiction to biography. Any suggestions for books you would like to see in large print or audio are always welcome. Please send to the Editorial Department at:

ISIS Publishing Limited
7 Centremead
Osney Mead
Oxford OX2 0ES

A full list of titles is available free of charge from:
Ulverscroft Large Print Books Limited

(UK)
The Green
Bradgate Road, Anstey
Leicester LE7 7FU
Tel: (0116) 236 4325

(Australia)
P.O. Box 314
St Leonards
NSW 1590
Tel: (02) 9436 2622

(USA)
P.O. Box 1230
West Seneca
N.Y. 14224-1230
Tel: (716) 674 4270

(Canada)
P.O. Box 80038
Burlington
Ontario L7L 6B1
Tel: (905) 637 8734

(New Zealand)
P.O. Box 456
Feilding
Tel: (06) 323 6828

Details of **ISIS** complete and unabridged audio books are also available from these offices. Alternatively, contact your local library for details of their collection of **ISIS** large print and unabridged audio books.